JILLEEN DOLBEARE

Splintered Veil

VINCI
BOOKS

By Jilleen Dolbeare

Splintered Magic

Vinci Books

vinci-books.com

Published by Vinci Books Ltd in 2025

1

Printed and bound in Great Britain by Clays Ltd, Elcograf S.p.A.

Chapter One

I turned the kettle on for hot water and put dry cocoa mix in my mug. This was my first time out of bed in three days. The witches had done a number on me. I'd been beaten within an inch of my life, and although I wasn't a doctor, I bet my ribs were cracked, and my jaw was broken. The only reason I was up was because my cat had threatened me with a mouse. I didn't have the energy to take care of a dead rodent, and I definitely didn't for a living one.

Megan texted that she was close. Only the desire to see her and feel the comfort of her presence kept me from going back to bed. I'd cleaned up and gingerly washed my tender face. There wasn't anything I could do with my hair, so I twisted it into a messy bun, where it wouldn't bug me. Even my hair hurt. That might have been because a male witch had dragged me across a clearing by my hair and used it to throw me into an altar. I'm sure several hunks of hair were missing. I couldn't bear to look.

Gravel crunched outside. I hobbled to my kitchen door as I followed the sound around back, stepping out onto the porch. Excitement and relief filled my broken body. Megan waved at me from her SUV. I started to wave back, but the pain in my back and my ribs screamed, and I yanked my hand down quickly. She didn't notice. Damn those witches and their evil agenda.

Megan bounced out of the driver's side and opened the back door, reaching into the back seat for her bag and a pillow. She turned and rushed to my back porch.

Her dark hair was in a high ponytail, and her favorite sweats encased her shapely figure. I would have grinned at the sight, but my face hurt too much. I groaned. I didn't even have a place for her to sleep. She could spend a few nights with me in my bed, but I'd have to order a mattress for her. I was a terrible friend.

She flounced over the gravel and up the stairs to the porch. She finally looked up at me and gasped.

"Oh my God, Brigid. What happened?" She tossed her things down and wrapped me in a careful hug.

I burst into tears. She held me awhile as I sobbed. After what must have been forever, I calmed down. She let me go, and I invited her into the house. She gathered up her things and followed me into the kitchen. I must have inadvertently called Mr. Mittens, or he was hungry. Either way, he met us there and leaped gracefully up onto the table. Megan jumped back.

"That scared me," she said, then noticed the cat. "Oh my, what a gorgeous cat!"

He was beautiful—long creamy fur with blue-grey points and two front white mittens.

He blinked at her with enormous periwinkle blue eyes and m'rowed. Then he leaned in for her to scratch his ears and give him a thorough pet.

I wasn't sure how to explain what had happened

without first telling her about magic. Since she was as unlikely to believe he could talk as I had been at first, I needed something to assist me. It would be awesome if Mr. Mittens could talk to her.

That gave me an idea. I told Megan to wait there and hobbled my way to the bathroom, where I picked up the charm I'd made to protect her. I held it and focused my magic on it, telling it to allow her to hear magical creatures. And the pendant flashed.

I took it back to the kitchen. She was still petting my cat, who appeared to be in ecstasy. The harlot.

"Hold out your hand," I said.

She looked at me curiously. "Okay." She held out her hand.

I dropped the necklace into her open hand.

"What's this?" she asked and studied it. "Is it Alexandrite?"

I gave a very small smile, my face aching. "Yes, I know you love it."

She tried to hand it back. "I can't take it. That's a large stone and I know how much you spent on it."

"You're wrong. I didn't spend one dime on it. It was my grandmother's," I said, proudly. I knew she wouldn't take it if I'd spent too much money on her.

Her face twisted up in horror, and she thrust the necklace at me. "Now, I really can't take it!"

"Why not?"

"It's part of your inheritance. You can't give me something that was your grandmother's!"

I pushed her hand back towards her. "She left me a ton of jewelry. This wasn't even close to the most expensive piece, so you can take it without any guilt. Please take it. It'll make me happy."

She took it back, reluctantly.

"Please put it on," I encouraged. Then I stood up and walked behind her so I could help her with it. She looped it around her neck and handed me the ends. I fastened them.

I sat back down. My breath rasped, my knees and arms were weak, and I felt like I'd been kicked again. Everything must have shown on my face because Megan looked concerned, then asked me again what'd happened.

I took a moment and caught my breath. Feeling better prepared because she was wearing the charm, I started my tale from the moment I'd arrived until now, focusing mainly on how the witches had played me, stolen my magic, beaten me to a pulp, and then taken Gabe. Megan let me continue without interruption, although her face betrayed every emotion and her disbelief. Once I was done, she stood up and began pacing.

"I know you don't believe me. But I can prove it." I looked at my cat, who had splooted over the table throughout my whole retelling. "Mr. Mittens, you're up."

He gave me a bored, blue-eyed gaze. *What do you wish me to do?* He spoke into my mind.

"I imbued Megan's necklace with the power to hear you. Please, speak to her," I said.

He turned his face to her. I watched her as she heard him speak into her mind. Her eyes flew open wide, and she sat back down, hard.

"What?" she gasped.

I knew I hadn't believed the cat was speaking the first time, so I turned to him and asked out loud, "I think maybe you should show her your true form."

As you wish.

He hopped lightly to the floor and found an area big enough to transform.

Megan yelped and leapt onto my table. I probably should have warned her. "That's, that's…" She pointed at my cat. "A saber-toothed tiger!"

I giggled, then coughed, as the movement was like a new kick in the ribs. Not only did he not look like pictures on the internet I'd seen of saber-toothed tigers, but Mr. Mitten's expression was disgusted at the implication he could possibly look like something so lowly and earthbound as a saber-toothed tiger. This time, he spoke to both of us.

I'm most certainly not, he huffed. *I am a Splintercat.*

His four hundred plus pound shape filled my large kitchen. He looked a little like a gigantic bobcat. He had a round pumpkin-shaped head with four-inch canines that hung from his top jaw to below his bottom jaw. His front end was a little higher than his back end; he wasn't as long bodied as wild earth cats, although he looked balanced. He was spotted like a jaguar, had tufted ears like a Maine Coon, and had a bobbed tail that was approximately a foot long. He twitched it in irritation at Megan. His eyes remained a blazing periwinkle blue.

Hmpf. He snorted with disgust, then morphed back into his Ragdoll shape and wandered out of the kitchen.

Megan climbed down and returned to her chair. "Magic is real."

"Yup."

"Wow."

"Yup."

I couldn't say much else. She needed some time to process and accept. Her hand drifted up to the necklace, and she grasped the stone and slid it along the chain, her face blank, staring into nothing.

After a few minutes, she looked at me. "So, this necklace does what?"

"Well, I imbued it with the pieces of magic I have. Hopefully it will protect you from almost all magic but ice, air, aether, reality and time."

"OK."

"Don't take it off. I have no idea what the witches will do if they know you're here."

She nodded.

I knew she needed a break. This was a lot. It had taken me several days to absorb the truth.

"Do you want to tell me why you brought a trailer?" I asked.

She grinned. "I finally did it. I quit my job and told that bastard ex of yours to take a giant leap."

A wave of relief washed over me. I'd begged her to do this from the moment I told Evan I wanted a divorce. I knew he'd do everything in his power to punish her once I was out of his reach.

"I've come to throw myself on your good nature and be your slave for life. You only have to support me until I find a new job." She smiled uncertainly as she spoke.

I knew that was hard for her to say and do. She hated being beholden to anyone. But at the same time, my heart swelled with happiness. I had my best friend! I'd support her forever just to have her close to me again.

"Trust me, I'm dancing a jig on the inside," I said. "And you already have a job."

"I do?" she asked, confused.

"Yes, I'm starting a new business, and you are in on the ground floor. I think that immediately makes you vice president."

"Yay! I demand a raise."

We both giggled.

"Well, you can only go up from zero," I said.

"True. What's the business? I probably should ask before I make my new business cards."

"I'll show you later. It's in the same field, so you'll fit into the work environment perfectly. You'll do great around the water cooler."

"So glad. I don't want to be the odd woman out."

"Too true, but since the other employees are a Splintercat and a griffin, you're already the odd one."

She laughed, a little wild eyed, but still she laughed.

She sobered up quickly once it was clear that laughing hurt me. "We'll talk about the business later," she said. "First, let's take care of you. Your face could have broken bones in it. We really should take you to the doctor."

"No." I started to shake my head but thought better of it. "I can't go anywhere. I don't know who the witches are, or where they'll show up. I think one or more might work at the clinic."

She opened her mouth to protest. I held up my hand. I took a breath. I couldn't sustain long speeches since I couldn't take deep breaths. "Plus, I need to find Gabe first. He's still missing. He might be worse off than me. I have no way of knowing. The werewolves are looking, but they don't have the magic to help if it comes to another fight."

When she didn't look convinced, I continued. "If I find him and he's alright, he can heal me. If he's not, I'll go to Portland or somewhere to get looked at. I promise."

She gave me a judgmental look, trying to decide if I was lying or not. I must have passed because she nodded. "OK for now. But we need to do something soon."

I needed to change the subject before she had me agreeing to something I didn't want to agree to. "So, what's in your trailer? You didn't have time to pack everything!"

She smiled. "Naw. I packed the essentials. Frankly, just

everything I wanted to keep. I hired a company to empty the house, either junk what's left or sell it. When they're done, I'm selling the house. I'm out of there!"

"Wow, when you make a decision, you go all out," I said.

"I took my cue from you. You were out in what, a week?" She knew; she'd helped me pack. I'd done much the same thing. Packed what I wanted, had a junker do the rest, and sold the place remotely.

"Something like that."

"So, when we decide, we move on. That's what I did." She threw up her hands in excitement.

"Cool. I don't know if I can help you right now, though."

"Nothing is too heavy. There's no furniture, just keepsakes and some books. I can haul it in without help."

"I don't have a room for you yet, but you can choose one. I still have to order the mattresses for the finished rooms."

"No worries, I can crash on the floor."

"You can sleep with me until the mattress gets here. It's a king-size bed. Although Mr. Mittens still manages to take most of it."

She laughed and shrugged. "Whatevs."

"I don't know if the workers will come back and finish." I sighed. "There isn't much left to do, at least."

"They better not come back, not after the stunt the witches pulled and that bastard Scott. I can't believe you took him back after he gave you the potion."

Sofia, the head witch, had installed her cousin as the head of my renovation team after she'd murdered the local werewolf alpha and head of Whelan Restoration, who'd originally been working on my old Victorian house. Then, she'd mixed up a love potion to keep me enamored of Scott and distracted so they could steal the missing pieces of my magic. All of that culminated in my current state when I'd tried to stop her.

"I know," I said. "But I had to get the house finished. I couldn't find anyone else to do it in less than a year. Now, the jobs left are so small, I could probably get a small-time contractor here and there to finish. Just some painting, and some finish electric and plumbing. All the big stuff is done."

"Cool, the outside of the house is gorgeous. I love the paint scheme. Can't wait until you get the landscaping done."

It was beautiful. I'd had it painted in classic Victorian colors—dark green, dark red, and tan.

"Yeah, it'll be a showstopper." I sighed again. I just saw more work. But I'd signed up for it. "Ready to see the inside?"

"If it looks as good as this kitchen, I can't wait!"

I wanted to be out looking for Gabe. However, the wolves were on it, and I was still too injured. I needed another day to recover or more. If I was honest with myself, it would probably be weeks. At least I kept telling myself just one more day so I could enjoy Megan and the comfort she brought with her presence.

"OK. The second you see the room you want, let me know. It's yours. Don't just choose one because it's finished. Promise?"

"Sure. I can share for a while to get the perfect room." She looked at me oddly.

I didn't think she'd choose a room just because it was finished. I wanted her to know she didn't have to settle. I had a room I thought she'd like, but I didn't want her to say no because it was the best room besides mine. If she knew I planned to turn this into a bed-and-breakfast someday, she might choose the smallest room or the ugliest. I'd have to nudge her in the right direction. I thought I'd turn the second-floor primary bedroom into an apartment by closing off the turret and the unfinished room on that end. Now that she was here, I wanted her to have her own space. I smiled in delight.

"Let's start on the third floor and make our way down." I stood up painfully, and hobbled, bent over, to the back of the kitchen and the stairs.

Megan gasped in alarm. "Can you do the stairs in your condition?" She hurried over and reached for my elbow to help.

"I don't have to. I have an elevator," I said, proudly.

"Seriously? That's so cool."

I led her out of the kitchen to the elevator door under the grand staircase. She released my arm and walked around the entryway, looking up.

"This entryway is amazing," she said as she gazed all about, her face looking up at the top of the house.

"I know. I'm going to find the biggest Christmas tree in the state and put it in here," I said.

"Can't wait to see that!"

"Me either."

I hit the button, and the door swished open. It wasn't a large elevator. Big enough for two people and a couple of suitcases. So, we were comfortable on the short ride to the third floor. We came out at the top of the staircase. I started her down toward the end of the hall by the attic entrance. The door was standing open.

"Is that the infamous attic?"

"Sure is. I'd take you up there, but it's just more stairs and storage. So maybe later when I feel better."

"No worries. I don't need to see it now."

We opened the first door to a new suite. The rooms up here were mostly finished, although the furniture was a jumble, and the finish plumbing needed to be completed. But they were formed, and the beauty was showing through.

"Wow," Megan exclaimed after each room. She adored the turret room as well, and that made me smile.

We took the elevator down to the second floor. It was only my second or third time using it, and I was happy it ran smoothly and quietly. Again, we started at the room furthest from the turret room and made our way around.

"These rooms are mostly finished; except I have an idea that's going to need a little more work." I looked at her from the corner of my eye.

She just nodded.

I had my furniture pieces in each room, although none were arranged, and the beds didn't have mattresses. The bathrooms were all finished, and most had been cleaned of all the construction dust and debris.

"These are so beautiful!" she exclaimed at each room with its individual paint scheme. Finally, the third suite door was ahead of us, next to the turret. She had gushed over the turret, and I smiled. Then, I let her open the door and step inside the room I thought would be her favorite.

She gasped. The room was done in seafoam green, and all the wood was painted white. Every other room had natural wood, refinished and stained. Here, I had all the wood done in gleaming high gloss white. The floor was still the original oak, refinished to a high gleam. The furniture that was in the room was also white. It needed a good cleaning and probably new paint, but you could see the bones and what this room could be. The bathroom was magnificent. Almost a twin to mine. The original claw-footed tub from this floor had been re-enameled, and everything inside the bathroom was gleaming white marble. The new modern glass shower had a million shower heads and was large enough for four people. It was a dream bathroom.

"I love it! This is the room!"

I smiled. "I knew it."

She jumped up and down a little.

"There's still some work to be done. If you like this room, which you do, how about we enclose it with the turret and make a little apartment? You'd have a sitting room or reading nook and the bed and bathroom. We'd still have to share the kitchen, but what do you think?"

I stumbled a little through the speech; I wanted her to love the house and to stay so much. It was still a good idea even if she wanted to leave eventually, because enclosing the turret would make this a larger space for families. I could add a pull-out couch or something if Megan ever left.

She squealed with delight. "You really want me to stay?"

"More than anything."

"Yes, yes, yes!" And she did a little happy dance.

I laughed. "I'm so happy. I'd dance with you, but I'd probably not survive."

"I'll bring all my stuff up here. Is the bathroom ready to be used?"

"Yeah, the water is hooked up and everything works."

"I'd sleep up here if there was a mattress." She looked around.

"Well, all the furniture needs a wash and paint. We can order the mattress of your dreams tonight. And by the time it gets here, we should have the furniture all done."

"Perfect."

We both looked around.

"So, what do you have for food? I'm starving."

"Me too." I frowned. "How about we order something? I haven't felt up to cooking."

"Whatever you choose, I can go pick it up if they don't deliver out here."

"I know who delivers." I gave her a list of choices, and we made a decision and ordered.

While we waited, she started to unload her tiny trailer. She really hadn't brought much. Every piece of luggage she owned was full, and maybe ten to twelve additional boxes and totes. She brought things in and loaded the elevator.

I felt bad I couldn't help, but she was so happy to be here, she kept telling me not to worry about it.

I helped her organize her bath things. She was thrilled with the beautiful bathroom and declared she could live in it. I smiled.

After everything was done, we went back to the kitchen. The food was late, luckily, since it gave us time to get her stuff organized. She would have to live out of a suitcase until we got the furniture squared away. Her closet was finished, but it also needed the construction dust cleaned out before she unpacked her clothes.

The pizza finally arrived. I put out salad and soda, and we tucked in. Megan had the disgusting habit of dipping her pizza in ranch dressing. I shuddered.

"Do you have a plan to find Gabe?" Megan asked as we ate.

I put my slice down. I'd done nothing but think about this. "First, we have to find him and figure out what the witches have done to him." My appetite had disappeared as the anxiety and worry built up in my gut.

"They probably have him in chains in a dungeon somewhere," she said.

I blinked at her. "No. They can't do that. He's a doctor.

13

An upstanding community member. They'll let him go when they're done," I explained. Not sure why I was so positive. It just made sense. This was a small town. Maybe five thousand people lived here. A missing doctor would be noticed.

She shook her head. "No way. How else would they control him? They can't just let him go. He'll tell on them. Get them arrested for kidnapping, get a restraining order. I'm telling you, they're keeping him in chains somewhere."

"Those are good points." I shook my head. "But you're forgetting something. It's easy to do, I struggled with it too. Magic."

"What do you mean by 'magic'?"

"They can do something to control him with magic." After what I'd told her about everything that had happened and witnessing Mr. Mittens' transformation, I was confused at her inability to grasp what magic could do.

"What?"

"That's the scary part, I don't know. I'm very much a noob at this. And I don't know much about witch magic. But after what I've seen them do, they aren't limited by scruples."

"Yeah, I guess not." She looked me up and down, all beaten and bruised as I was.

"I didn't mean just what they did to me, I meant what they did to Craig Whelan and the stuff with the love potion."

"I know," she said.

"So how do a human and a Fae lord go about freeing a hot doctor from a bunch of unscrupulous witches?"

I sighed. "I'm not a real Fae lord. My cat just likes to mess with me."

"Come on, let me have this! It's so cool, like a fantasy story or something."

"I'm going to regret telling you that, aren't I?"

"Yes, yes, you are."

"You are so lucky I love you, or I'd Fae lord your ass."

"Sounds kinky." She winked at me.

"Ugh, go dunk something in ranch dressing."

She looked at me and dunked her last bite of pizza in the ranch and shoved it in her face. She was trying to act seductive, but she ended up missing slightly and smearing ranch over her mouth and cheek. Then, we both cracked up, and she spewed ranch covered pizza bits all over the table. I grabbed my ribs firmly but couldn't stop laughing.

After we cleaned up the mess and the remains of dinner, she said she was going upstairs to break in her new bathroom.

I assumed that meant taking a bath or shower, so I nodded. After she left the kitchen, I pulled out my laptop and started looking for mattresses. I found and bookmarked a few for Megan to look over. After that was done, I pulled up the proposal for my new business and emailed it to her. With nothing else to do, I started googling all I could on witches. I needed to be better prepared, or as prepared as possible.

I couldn't find anything to help me. I should have guessed. I needed a witch in my pocket, but I couldn't trust the witches around here, and probably not any witches anywhere.

Megan came down as I was pounding swear words into my laptop in frustration. She laughed when she saw what I was doing. It was something I'd done to avoid swearing at Evan when we were married. He didn't think swearing was dignified. Which generally meant that swearing at *him* was disrespectful. I don't think he understood the point of getting cussed out.

It used to be my only way of expressing my frustration, but it wasn't working at the moment. Now, I could scream cuss words at the sky, but no one cared. But it wasn't solving my problem of finding or saving Gabe.

I still had the gut feeling that they would turn him loose to go back to his life after some heavy spell layering. I just had to wait it out. I could check on him. I knew where he lived and worked. Tomorrow, I'd call his work. If he was missing, I'd go to his house. I told Megan the plan, and she agreed. Exhausted, we went to bed.

Mr. Mittens curled tightly against me—his warmth and security a comfort. Megan snored lightly. I thought I'd fall instantly asleep having done more today than I had in days, but instead, I stared into the dark, eaten up with worry about Gabe and what the witches were doing to him.

Chapter Two

The second I knew the clinic opened, I called. Eight a.m. sharp. The receptionist answered with a sleepy good morning. I told her I wanted to set an appointment with Dr. Ambrose. She was quiet for a moment. My heart raced. He had to be there; he had to be okay.

"Dr. Ambrose doesn't have an open appointment this week. Would you like to see someone else?" she asked.

"No, I'd really prefer Dr. Ambrose. Is he out of town?" I prompted.

"No, he was out sick for a couple of days, but he's back now, just behind. If you like, I can add you to his cancellation list."

"No, I'll call back. I need to think about it." Relief caused me to slump as all my tension dissipated. He wasn't free of the witches, of that I was sure, but he wasn't in chains in a dungeon like Megan believed.

The receptionist probably thought I was nuts. You either needed a doctor or you didn't. It wasn't a dinner reservation.

I ended the call and looked up at Megan who was sipping coffee with her feet up on the chair and one arm around her knees.

"Gabe's at work."

"Well, blow me down."

I laughed. "Yeah." She'd picked up that saying from me.

"So, are you going to go see him?" she asked.

"No, I couldn't get an appointment. But I'm wondering if I should go to his house later."

I thought of his SUV still parked behind my house. I wondered what he was driving and what the witches told him about the missing car. Otherwise, why wouldn't he have retrieved it? Weird.

"You should. We both should."

I looked at her, assessing. "You just want to check him out."

"I never!" She flipped her long hair back. "I resemble that remark."

"Yes, you do."

We laughed. The relief of joking with my bestie helped ease the knot in my stomach.

"I just want to make sure he's *fine…*"

I threw her the look.

"I mean, uh, alright." She grinned.

"I know what you meant."

"So, now that Gabe is tooken. What other hot men have you found in town? I gotta catch up to you."

Her body language was still tense, worried, even if her tone was light. Bless Megan. She knew I was terrified of whatever the witches had done to him, and she was doing her darndest to take my mind off it. I gave her a grateful smile.

"Scott is the only one I've met, but you want to avoid

him like the plague." I thought for a moment. "The Whelan brothers are pretty fine. I don't know if they're involved or married, though. And they're a little younger. At least two of them are closer to our age, but I'm not sure exactly."

"Intriguing. Werewolves, huh?"

"Yes."

"Are they hairy?"

"What?"

"Like do they look a little on the wild and wolfy side when they're human?" She wiggled her eyebrows.

"No, they look like men." I yawned. I wasn't quite ready to be awake, the yawn made my sore jaw ache and grind. Darn, it was most likely broken. "Fine, muscular, dreamy men." I fluttered my eyelashes at her. That was the only thing that had fully recovered. My eyelashes. My eyelids still hurt though, part of the joy of two black eyes. Joking helped my heart, if not my aching body. I could forget my worries for a moment.

"Why didn't you get a doctor's appointment?" she asked after watching me wince and rub my face.

"I only want one with Gabe."

Megan had her stubborn look on. "Well, you should have made one even if it's for later, tell them you want in if there's a cancellation."

"OK, Mom."

She watched to make sure I called back. I made the appointment and asked for anything that came open earlier, the receptionist put me on the list, and that was that.

"See, that was easy. If you get him to heal you before that, you can cancel."

I started to roll my eyes, but I was afraid one might fall out, so I didn't.

"I'm going to go get us some breakfast," Megan announced.

"What? Why? I have food here we can make," I protested.

"Do you feel up to making it?" she asked, hands on her hips.

"No, not really."

"This is my treat to you and myself. I just got here and I'm not ready to work. I need a mini vacay. Plus, I have to return the trailer."

"Fair enough."

She grabbed her purse and borrowed my rain jacket since it had started to drizzle again. She wasn't prepared for this much rain.

I left her a note that I was soaking in the bath in case she came back before I finished, which was likely. Then, I went to soak away some of the pain. When I saw myself in the bathroom mirror without my clothes, it scared me a little. I was so black and blue from the beatings, that if I'd seen someone else like this, I'd have notified the police and taken them to the ER.

I didn't want those damned witches to know how bad I was hurt though, and I couldn't trust them to not be every-where I wanted to be. I hadn't seen enough faces, but there had been so many of them they could be anywhere or everywhere in this town. I'd told Megan that was one of the reasons why I didn't want to go to the clinic or the hospital. I thought I'd recognized a witch I'd seen at one of those places. I shuddered. But that hurt. I ran the water as hot as I could handle, dumped in an entire bag of Epsom salts, and slid down into the glorious tub.

I woke up when Megan grabbed me and hauled me to the surface.

"What are you doing!" I yelled when the water cleared out of my eyes.

Megan's eyes were wild, her face flushed. "You were underwater. I thought you'd drowned!"

I blinked. "I was fine." This was new. I'd been underwater, and I didn't know for how long. Could my water magic help me breathe underwater? Did I grow gills or something? I reached up and felt my face and throat. Everything felt the same.

Megan sank down on the fluffy rug next to the tub, her breathing ragged. "This was another magic thing, wasn't it?"

"I don't know. I have no idea how long I was under. How long were you gone?"

She looked at her phone. "About forty-five minutes."

I felt my heart skip a beat. I remembered about five minutes of being in the bath. I may have been under for nearly forty minutes.

"I think it may be a magic thing. I think I was under there a lot longer than a couple of minutes."

I had her hand me a towel, and I stepped out of the tepid water and let it drain. I dried off and wrapped my long auburn hair in a towel and myself in my robe. *Mr. Mittens*, I thought loudly. I knew he could sense me on this land and hear me just fine.

Sure enough, a couple minutes later, Megan and I were seated at the table with our breakfast when he strolled in.

You bellowed?

I laughed, and Megan looked at me. "I was laughing at him." I pointed at the cat, my mouth half full. I finished my mouthful. "Do you have your necklace on?"

Her hand darted to her neck, which was bare. She paled. "No, I took it off last night when I took a bath. I'll be right back."

She dashed off, her steps pounding loudly up the stairs. She came back wearing the necklace.

"Now, you can hear Mr. Mittens," I said, trying not to reprimand her after I'd practically begged her to wear it all the time.

Are you ready to tell me why you called? he asked drolly.

"I fell asleep in the tub."

He blinked his large blue eyes at me, waiting for more of the story.

"Underwater."

His eyes opened ever so slightly larger.

"For forty minutes."

He blinked. *That is interesting.*

"Yes, do you know why I'm not dead?"

Magic?

"Very funny. Do you know how it works?"

I don't. You keep asking me about your magic. I'm not a magical Fae *cat.*

"I know, but you've been around a long time, and you've seen more than I have."

Hmpf.

"Did my grandmother ever hang out underwater?"

Not that I'm aware of. She may not have known this aspect of her power, or she wasn't as strong as you are.

"Oh well, I guess I don't have to worry about it unless I fall asleep in the bathtub again."

Is that all, my pet? he said with a large yawn.

Megan's eyes flew open. "Pet?"

"Yeah, it's our thing. I'm his charge. He likes to call me his pet."

"Hey, before we go check out your doctor tonight, can I meet your griffin friend?" Megan asked.

Mr. Mittens looked at me, so I waved him away to let him know we were done. Of course, that was after a chin scratch and an ear rub. He wandered off.

"Sure, why not."

I walked out to the porch and called for Brightfeather. Brightfeather had explained to me that she heard my calls and would came as quickly as she could, so I didn't worry when she didn't show up immediately. She would come as soon as she was able. We drank our coffee out on the back porch, watching the rain—me in my robe with my hair in a towel, and Megan in her sweats. By the time we were finishing up, a great, grey eagle drifted in and landed on the porch railing.

Hello, Lady Brigid. Is all well with you?

"Yes, Brightfeather. Is all well with you?"

Yes, thank you. How may I serve you?

That woke me up more than my coffee. I didn't need a servant. I thought of Brightfeather as a friend.

"Umm, you don't have to serve me, Brightfeather. I just wanted to introduce you to another of my friends." I gestured to Megan. "This is Megan. She is human and doesn't have magic, but I want you to know that you can show your true self to her. She knows everything." I turned to Megan. "Megan, this is my dear friend, Brightfeather. She is a magnificent griffin. She is not my servant, but my friend," I said pointedly.

Brightfeather shifted into her real form, and Megan gasped. She stood and looked as though she was going to reach out and pet the griffin. I put my hand out, but she stopped herself, realizing that it was rude to pet a sentient creature, unless it was a ridiculous Splintercat who liked to walk around as a Ragdoll.

Brightfeather looked a little off balance since I'd made it clear she wasn't a servant of the Fae lord of the land. I wanted to swat my cat a little for telling everyone that—but not too much, because he could remove my head with one claw.

Brightfeather, with her courtly manners, dipped her head in a bow to Megan, and spoke into our minds. *I'm pleased to meet you.*

"You are the coolest creature I've ever met," Megan gushed.

Thank you, Brightfeather preened.

I laughed. "You are amazing, and thank you for helping the other night, you saved my life."

It is my pleasure. I have sanctuary and freedom on your land. It is a small price to pay for such a gift.

I bowed my towel-covered head to her. "It is a small gift; I wish I had more to offer you. I do want you to think of us as friends."

Thank you, I like having you as a friend, Lady Brigid.

She gave us a respectful bow, then shifted back into her eagle form and launched herself from the porch and out over the woods.

"What else do you have in your woods?" Megan asked after Brightfeather disappeared from view.

"Umm, bears. Lots of dead invaders apparently, unless Mr. Mittens eats them. I'm afraid to ask. The only one I know that is friendly is Brightfeather. I think there may be other supernatural creatures out there, but I haven't met them. My cat is the boss of that." I waved away the question with a flick of my hand.

"Your life has seriously gotten weird."

"Yet, it finally feels right for some strange reason."

We sat in silence for a while.

"I know you told me your story, but how do you find the rest of your magic?" Megan asked.

"I don't know. I have my gram's description of the objects that contained her power, so I have an idea of what form they might take, but I've searched the house multiple times, and I don't think they're here or know where they could be. I also don't know for sure what they do. Time and air seem self-explanatory, but what does aether and reality do? It's confusing. Plus, how do I get back my ice magic from that bitch of a witch? I'm out of my league. I also don't know what to do about Gabe. If he were still fully himself, he'd call or come get his car or something. I don't know what the witches did to him or if I can undo it. I wish I had someone to talk to!"

"I know I'm not much, but I'm here." She reached over and grabbed my hand and gave it a squeeze. "Here's an out of the box thought." She stood, put her coffee cup on the railing and faced me. "Your cat said that your great-grand-father, the Fae lord, could live for thousands of years. Couldn't he help you?"

A frisson of shock ran through me. I hadn't even thought of him. He would know everything about my magic. He used to come here years ago to visit his wife and daughter. Would he see me? Had he been here since she died? I had no way of knowing. But there was one problem. "I don't know how to contact him."

"You said you had your grandmother's journals. Didn't she contact him? Could she have left instructions, even unknowingly, in her diaries?"

"Huh. I have some journals, true. I haven't noticed anything in them like that. But we could look in the attic and see if we can find more."

I finally had something, a plan to help me and help Gabe. We looked at each other, then dashed into the house. Well, Megan dashed, I hobbled, but the intent was there. I left my coffee mug on the table and shuffled to the elevator. Megan took the stairs. I met her at the attic door.

"That is so cool!"

"What?" I asked.

"The door didn't appear until you were like three feet away from it." I'd closed it on our first foray up here.

"I forgot for a moment, of course, it only shows up when it senses me or my magic, not sure which."

"Didn't it show up before you got your powers?"

"Yeah, but Mr. Mittens seems to think I have some inherent magic even without my active powers."

"Oh."

"It's not important. It works, if someone needs to get up there, I can leave the door open like it was the first time we came by."

She shrugged. We climbed the few attic stairs and stood in the vast space. She gasped.

"Wowzer."

I laughed.

"I bet all this antique furniture is worth a fortune."

"It might be, but I was hoping to use most of it to furnish the house. I've sold a few pieces already, I know I sold them too cheaply, but they're gone, and I don't have to worry about them. I had to make room for the elevator equipment."

She made a beeline for the old trunks. "These are so neat."

"Yeah, but I've already searched them. I haven't done much in the back; we should start there."

She nodded, and we wove our way to the back through the stacks of old furniture and boxes of who knew what. I hadn't done any work in the back. I'd gone there and felt around to see if any of my magic called to me, but it hadn't. I hadn't looked through any boxes and just marked furniture to be removed for sale. There could be journals back here. There weren't any more trunks, but plenty of boxes.

"I haven't searched the furniture or boxes back here," I said after we were at the back wall. I'd also called some books to me before—my grandmother's journals. I doubted anything from her was left. I had no idea if my great-grandmother had even written journals.

"Let's get started," Megan said, the light of the hunt sparking in her eyes. She actually rubbed her hands together in glee. I had forgotten how much she enjoyed antiquing. This must look like heaven to her.

"If you see anything you want for your room, just tell me."

"Oh, I will."

We each chose a box and got started.

Several hours later, we were grubby, grumpy, and thoroughly sick of antiques. We did have several more books to search through, though. But first, we had an appointment at Gabe's house.

We showered, dressed, and met downstairs to head to his house. I had Megan drive her car, and I drove Gabe's car. That was our excuse, we were returning it.

I led the way, and she followed carefully. Of course, it

was pouring rain, and my thick, wavy hair, that I'd carefully smoothed and tamed, was now a floofy frizzball. But it didn't matter since half my face was swollen and black and blue, gradually changing to purple, yellow, and green as well. I was lovely.

I wasn't sure how I felt as we pulled behind his house. His spare truck was there, so he had to be home. My guts were cramping, my hands were sweating, and my throat was closing off. I stepped out of the car nervously, his keys clutched in my hand. Megan followed me to the back door. I looked at her for reassurance and knocked. Footsteps echoed, coming gradually closer, then he was at the door. He looked down on us with an inquisitive smile on his face.

My heart stopped.

"Hi, can I help you?" he asked.

I'd been looking away, the ugly half of my face hidden by my hair. I turned and looked up at him. He was perfect. His handsome face was unmarked and unbruised. His brown hair dusted with a little silver at the sides was slightly mussed like he'd run his fingers through it. His hazel-green eyes were full of gentle kindness. He looked at me oddly. Like he was trying to remember who I was. Fear clawed its icy path down my back. What if he'd completely forgotten about me? How would I restore his memories?

"Wow, that's some bruise, what happened?" he asked. Frowning at me professionally.

"I was beaten by a bunch of witches," I answered truthfully.

His face filled with shock.

"Witches?" he repeated quietly.

"Yes, thank you for helping me. I brought your car back." I held my hand out with the keys in it.

"Car?" He sounded uncertain, drugged.

"Who are you?" he asked. "I know you, don't I?" He shook his head as though he were trying to dislodge something.

"Yes, I'm Brigid. Brigid Donovan." I gave him my maiden name. Maybe they hadn't tried to rewrite his *entire* memory.

"Brigid," he said uncertainly. "I think I used to know a Brigid."

He gestured for us to come in out of the rain.

Once we were in, boots and coats off and seated on his sofa, I tried to jar his memory.

"Yes, I'm Brigid, we used to date in high school. We started dating again recently."

He stopped me by putting up a hand. "That's not possible. I wouldn't date you. I have a girlfriend."

I jolted back in surprise. A girlfriend? My heart sank and my stomach clenched. No. That wasn't possible.

"Her name is Sofia; she's on her way over right now." He looked confused. "No, that isn't right." He put his hands to his head and closed his eyes tight. "If you ladies don't mind, I have a splitting headache." He stood and gestured for us to leave.

I reached over to hand him his car keys. "Here are your keys."

"Keys?"

"Yes, to your car? We brought it back from my house?"

"I don't have a car."

"You do, it's in the driveway. You can check the registration. It's yours."

He shook his head, then clenched his eyes shut again. I could tell he was in pain. Megan's eyes narrowed. She kept looking at him, then me. I felt like I'd been gut punched. I was on the edge of tears. He escorted us out and shut the door behind us.

Megan supported me as we walked to the car. My legs had gone weak and useless. Her face was grim and concerned.

We climbed into Megan's car, and she started the engine. We drove out in silence.

Chapter Three

I swallowed the lump that kept rising in my throat and focused on my rage. "That unbelievable, self-serving, witch whore," I said once the shock wore off, and I had control of my emotions.

Megan laughed. "You are definitely more relaxed away from Evan."

I smiled at her. "I guess you're right. But it's still true. She's put him under some spell, is trying to make herself his girlfriend, and made him forget me."

"I'd have gone with bitch whore, plus a few more," Megan said smugly. "So, what do we do?"

"We're going to do what we planned. We'll search those books, call up my great-grandpa, and use my magic to save Gabe from her claws. I have no choice. You saw what that spell was doing to him. Who knows if it will kill him, eventually? He's obviously fighting it."

She nodded. We'd already hurt him by exposing him to some truth, even if it was just a car and the fact his girlfriend wasn't Sofia, the raging bitch whore.

She'd wanted him, my house, and my magic for who knew how long. Maybe since high school. I can't believe I thought she was my friend. I pounded my hand on the dash and then moaned in pain. That movement hurt my hand, my ribs, and my back.

"So, what do you want to do to Sofia?" Megan asked after my outburst.

I opened my mouth to deliver all kinds of torments to the witch from hell, but before I could start, Megan stopped me by putting up a hand.

"Realistically." She threw me the side eye. "I know what you want to do. I'm sure that there are all kinds of torture and torments that you can dream up, but what can we do to her to make her pay, that we can get away with without doing twenty to thirty at the state pen?"

I closed my mouth. I hated reality. But Megan made sense. I wouldn't survive captivity. Just my hair would drive me mad without having the proper products. And I really doubted I'd get enough reading or computer privileges to satisfy me either. So, torture and murder were out—unless it was on my land where I could hide the body. I sighed.

"I just don't know. As a witch with Fae magic to power her, she's unstoppable. The only thing that keeps witches in check is the state of their magic—having a limit and having to be careful. She's beyond that now."

"Don't forget, you are Fae. You have that going for you. Plus, you have friends." She looked over at me. "You have more than one piece of Fae magic, what makes her stronger with only one?"

I looked at her. "She's not limited by morals. She's already a powerful witch, now she'll have years of power that won't drain her personal power well. Also, she has an entire coven, and she's taken Gabe, whose power added to hers is significant."

"So, your friend part is weak, but you do have a Splintercat," she added weakly.

"Yup, I have a cat, a griffin, part of a werewolf pack, an unfinished house, and a bestie. We're gonna win for sure." Despair welled up, and I almost lost control of my emotions again.

She slugged me lightly on the arm. "That's the spirit." I groaned dramatically, although it hadn't hurt much.

We were *so* going to die.

When we got back to the house, we took the books and searched through them. Right away, Megan found an interesting passage. The books were mixed. Some were my grandmother's, but the interesting one belonged to my great-grandmother—who'd been a witch. She was the one who'd found herself a Fae lord and married him.

Megan read the passage out loud. "'I found the spell book to summon a fairy. From what I've studied, the Fae folk can grant magic to a witch. This removes the risk of draining the witch's magic and will permanently eliminate the need to refill the witch's well.'"

She looked up at me. "This might be it, Brigid."

I nodded at her. "Keep going."

Megan continued to read from the journal, "'My parents kept the book hidden. I don't know why. If they had this, why haven't they used it? My mother is aging much too fast. She's using too much magic. When I capture the fairy, I'm going to demand it grant her magic first.'"

Megan stopped reading, and her eyes scanned the book. "There's a lot of stuff along this line, I'll skip ahead."

"K."

She scanned a few pages, moving her finger along the line as she read, then stopped. "'You must enter the forest and prepare the altar.'"

"Altar?" I asked, my mind racing. After the battle with the witches, I'd made the earth swallow the altar, and I'd hidden the clearing it had been in by telling the forest to swallow it up. Had I eliminated the one item I needed to call my great-grandfather forth? Could I pull the altar back from the earth I'd buried it in?

"Yeah, it says altar."

Would my great-grandmother have come to this land, which wasn't yet hers, to perform this ritual? Or did her family own some of it then? I didn't know. Mr. Mittens had told me that Fae gold had purchased this land. I shrugged. Not important. I needed a forest and an altar. I knew where to get them.

"OK, sorry I interrupted."

She nodded and continued, "'It would be best if the altar has a natural fairy ring, but if you can't find one, you can create a faux ring. Place items that are attractive to the fair folk in a ring around the altar and as offerings upon it. The Fae are partial to cream, honey, sweet cakes, and wine. Next, to protect yourself, make sure you have a ring of salt and iron around you. A fairy can be harmed by these items and is thus repelled by them.'"

She looked up at me. "Do you think she really did this? This ritual sounds fake."

"Don't forget that she married a Fae lord. Something worked."

"Yeah, I guess you're right." She shrugged and started

reading again, "Blah, blah, blah, sweets, ring of salt, ah this is where I was. 'After you are protected, wait for the full moon to hit its zenith. Then, prick your finger and allow three drops of blood to wet the altar and say these words. "Come to me fair one. Help me with this task. See me, obey me. Grant me what I ask."""

She looked up. "There's a page of symbols that you're supposed to add to the altar, and a page of motions you're supposed to perform as well."

"You're right, it sounds stupid." Disappointment took the wind out of my sails. This was a joke. We wouldn't even be able to call a pizza delivery with this stupid ritual. How was I going to save Gabe now?

She showed me the page of symbols.

"These don't look like anything to me but doodles. This can't be right," I said. Despair eating deeper into my psyche.

She agreed. "I'll keep reading. This sounds like a silly girl thing. But we know something worked, so maybe I'll find it."

I watched her read further, her brow wrinkled with concentration. A few moments later, she spoke. "It worked apparently. It's a real spell. Of course, she had her witch magic behind it, maybe that made the difference."

Something sparked in my mind. Excitement warmed my heart. Spells were just a way to focus your will and intent. Sofia had taught me that. So even if this spell sounded like a young girl's fanciful attempt, that young girl had the magic to back it up and make it work. I had the magic that would make it work. Confidence filled me.

"It'll work," I said suddenly.

Megan looked up from her book. "It will?"

"Yeah, you said it. She had the magic to make it

happen. And I have *his* magic. That has to be even more potent." I stood and paced. "Mark that page; we're gonna have a lot of work to do to recreate that ridiculous spell." I paced some more, thinking. "First, I have to raise an altar from the earth." Stupid me. Why did I bury it in the first place? "Plus, it's a walk—and not an easy one—I buried the clearing and caused the forest to regrow." I rubbed one of the sore, bruised spots on my back.

She marked the book and stood up. "Well, a walk is good for sore backs. Let's go check it out."

I sighed. I was sore, but she was right. You only healed if you kept moving. "OK."

We put on our mud boots and rain jackets, and I led her to the site of my failure—where I was beaten, lost my magic, and lost Gabe all in one night. At least it was rainy, muddy, and miserable to match my mood.

On top of that. I forgot to tell my cat, and I got us lost. It's amazing how one patch of forest looks like another. Before, there was a clearing—it was pretty obvious. Now, there was nothing.

"I know I saw that tree before," Megan said. "It has that patch of moss that looks like a T-Rex." She stepped toward the tree and reached out. "Especially now." She removed a tiny piece of moss near the T-Rex's mouth. Now, it really did look like a dinosaur.

I tilted my head to the right to get a better view. "Huh."

"Yeah."

"So, since you figured it out with your fantastic paleontology skills, you might as well know."

"Know what?"

"We're lost."

She rolled her eyes. "Yeah, I know." She sighed and removed another piece of moss from the T-Rex tree to make it even more obvious. "What do you do when you get lost in your own woods?"

"Well, the last time it happened, I swore that the next time I'd call my cat."

She raised an eyebrow. "Does he carry a phone?"

It took me a minute to decide if she was serious or making fun of me. I decided she really was confused. He did talk after all. "No, I just think at him, and he shows up."

She tensed. I saw her head come up and her gaze focused past my shoulder. "I hope he's fast, cause that is not good." She pointed.

I whirled around as fast as I could with my injuries. Coming at us was a real-life unicorn. And it was not what the fairy tales had told me. Propaganda. Just like Mr. Mittens warned me. It did have a single horn and the general appearance of an equine. But that's where the similarities ended.

"Get up a tree!" I yelled and stumbled towards a tree of my own. "Mr. Mittens!" I bellowed and prayed he was fast. His warnings raced through my mind as I grasped a branch and tried to haul myself up. But I was too injured. I couldn't force my body to work properly. I was spry for forty-two, and although I wasn't a gym rat, I fancied myself fairly fit.

Megan was already a third of the way up her tree. I couldn't even get up to the first branch of mine. I put the tree between me and the quickly approaching beast. Why had I wanted to see a real unicorn? Had I inadvertently brought it here to my woods with my wishing?

I tried to power up my injured magic. I could talk to animals, right? That was one of my powers. Did unicorns count as an animal or were they too *magical*? I concentrated my will and tried to connect to the raging creature as it galloped towards us—its eyes blazing red and its horn glowing with unholy fire. Shit, I'd never seen anything so terrifying. It wasn't as large as a regular horse, more pony sized, but it had clawed feet, not hooves, and it was eerily silent in its approach. Maybe climbing a tree wouldn't make a difference.

I didn't know if unicorns came in different colors. You always saw the perfectly white creature that represented purity. This one had black feet that faded up its body into white on its back, neck, and head. Its tail and mane were black. But it wasn't black in color, it was black fire. Its whole body and horn were blazing with a strange black fire. As it ran, it left little patches behind it that faded into real red and orange flame as it passed. I was lucky the woods were soaked or the whole forest would go up.

I looked around, trying to find an escape. But the unicorn was too fast, and soon, it was right on us. My magic did nothing against it, or it wasn't listening to me yell "stop" at it telepathically. I started yelling "stop" out loud, but that didn't help either. The unicorn was pissed. I had no idea why.

"What do you want?" I yelled in frustration since it wasn't listening to me yell, "Stop."

It slid to a stop just like a reining horse, rump down, back feet extended, front feet walking out to a complete stop. Then, it shook its head, and its flaming mane blazed high and hot, then faded out. It pranced around my tree and tried to poke me with its horn. It snorted, and flames shot out at me. I backed up in a panic and put another tree between us.

"Do you speak?" I pushed out with my magic.

The unicorn reared and pawed the air, its front claws glinting like knives in the light of its fading flames.

I do not speak to the filthy Fae. Its voice pierced my mind.

Great, a bigoted unicorn. Just what I needed—as if the horn, claws, and fire weren't terrifying enough.

Where was my cat? I threw a quick glance around, hoping to see him.

"Then, how do you explain what you want if you won't speak?" I asked the creature. I figured I'd either reason with it or delay it long enough so that Mr. Mittens could arrive and save us. Megan was all the way up the tree now.

"Brigid, get climbing!" She yelled down.

"I can't. I'm too hurt," I yelled up.

The unicorn charged at me again. I circled the tree, keeping the unicorn moving with me. It's unholy fire flaring up and causing the grass and fallen leaves around the tree to burst into flame. Since the flames were short lived in the damp, the smoldering leaves put out extra smoke, and I started to wheeze and cough.

"Mr. Mittens!" I coughed out the best I could, adding an extra burst of magic to the shout.

I'm coming. His gruff and put-out voice echoed in my mind.

A wave of relief flowed through me. I just had to keep the unicorn busy until he arrived. It couldn't take long, he always seemed to materialize when I called. I wondered what had kept him so long, although it couldn't have been more than a minute since I'd called him.

Another snort and burst of fire raged over me. This time, I felt the little hairs on my arms burn off, and I reached up to check my eyebrows. Still there. A wave of fury swept over me. I had fire magic, too, dammit. I almost called it up, but I stopped. This thing already used fire. It probably had defenses against fire magic. But I also had control of water, and between the rain and damp around us, there was plenty of water.

I focused my will and gathered up all the water I could hold and shot it at the unicorn. The water smacked it right in the face and washed over its body, drowning out the creature's natural flames. Just as I extinguished it, a giant cat launched itself through the air and landed on the unicorn's back. Razor-sharp claws grasping and teeth flashing as Mr. Mittens deployed them and gripped the back of the unicorn's neck. Mr. Mittens' weight, which I judged to be around four hundred pounds or more based on his size, pushed the unicorn's front end into the muddy earth.

The unicorn made a sound suspiciously similar to a roar, and using its powerful haunches, it lunged forward—awkwardly getting its front feet back under itself. Mr. Mittens ripped and tore at its back with his claws. The unicorn, having regained control of its legs, went down and rolled over Mr. Mittens trying to crush him with its weight. Even though it was pony sized, it still had to weigh close to a thousand pounds. It was solidly built. Muscles rippled, and unlike the propaganda, it was stout and stocky. It was closer to a tank than the waifish, delicate representations on tapestries I'd seen. I was beginning to wonder what happened to all those virgins the unicorns wanted to attract? I shuddered. It couldn't be good.

As it rolled, Mr. Mittens jumped clear between two trees. They were too close together, and now he had nowhere to go. If he tried to jump over the unicorn, it would gut him. If he ran forward, it would skewer him. He could back up, but I doubted he could do that fast enough, and he'd only be caught tighter between the trees. The unicorn charged.

I had to do something, or the evil beast would kill my cat. Terrified, I ran at the unicorn, approaching from the side. It would have to pass me to get at Mr. Mittens. I called to my magic with everything I had and lashed out with lightning.

The air crackled, and the woods lit up with a great flash. I couldn't see. Megan yelled out. I'd forgotten her. I hope the lightning didn't zap her, too. She was human, and I doubted she could survive a lightning blast without the talisman I'd made her. Leaf litter and dirt exploded around us. I closed my eyes. When I opened them, the unicorn lay twenty feet away. It had been knocked into a tree and stood slowly, acting disoriented. Its front feet were splayed and its head down. It breathed hard. Then, it shook its head and began to sort its feet.

Mr. Mittens growled. This time *he* charged the unicorn, and then in the last ten feet or so, he launched himself. His head was down as though he was going to ram the beast like a goat. Only, he sailed through the air, and when he hit the unicorn, it flew and slammed into a tree so hard, its body bent around the tree until its tail and head met. The snap of breaking bones filled the air, then the foul creature fell and lay crumpled on the ground, its fire snuffed—dead.

Mr. Mittens stood over it, his sides heaving. I noticed that the unicorn had gotten in a few blows—his sides were covered with deep, blood-dripping scratches. I stumbled over to him.

"You're wounded!" I reached out and grabbed his head and looked into his eyes. "Thank you."

The wounds are no matter. Here, on this land, I am the most powerful creature in this realm.

"You are magnificent," I said, stroking his ego. He'd earned it.

I watched his scratches. They were healing and looked old. The blood had stopped already.

Why are you in the woods without me? he asked, perturbed.

"I'm very sorry. I didn't mean to cause you trouble." I looked away. Megan was coming down the tree, and it wasn't gracefully. She was swearing like a sailor, and tree litter fell on us. "I wasn't thinking. We came to find the altar I buried and got lost. I was going to call you when the unicorn attacked us."

We both looked at the broken body of the evil beast. I shuddered. I didn't think any horse could scare me like the unicorn had. I never wanted to see another one. Why had I wished to see one?

Unicorns are dangerous, he reminded me.

"I see why you told me that."

"No shit," Megan added in, huffing and puffing from her exertion. A final crash told us she was down.

Hmpf. He reached back and licked some of the blood off his fur. The wounds were nearly closed. *How did you get lost in your own woods?* he asked casually as though he were amused.

"Well, it all looks the same."

You are the lord of this land. You should be able to go anywhere you desire with minimal effort. You are magical.

And an idiot, apparently. I never even considered using my magic or linking to my land to find my way. I blushed at my own stupidity. I guess Evan was right about me. I wasn't cut out to be a leader.

By then, Megan had picked herself up and joined us. "Why did a unicorn attack us?" she asked. Obviously confused and angry. Plus, her pants were torn, and she was covered in tree sap and bark.

Mr. Mittens turned his head to her but spoke into both of our minds. *Unicorns are the nastiest of all the creatures that inhabit this realm. You should avoid them.*

"I avoided alright. I haven't climbed a tree since I was fourteen." She brushed dirt off her clothing, frowning. "So, what do you do with the body? I don't think unicorn carcasses are common in this part of the world," Megan said. I could hear the irony in her voice.

I looked at Mr. Mittens. I still didn't know what he did with the creatures he killed, but I suspected he ate them. He nodded. I called on my earth power, and the earth pulled the carcass down until nothing remained.

"Wow." She stared at me. "I know you told me about your magic, but the lightning, and now that…" She pointed at where the carcass had lain. "That was freaking amazing!"

I smiled. Maybe I perked up on the inside, at least a little.

"So, I've seen you and your cat in action. I wish I hadn't been so freaked out. I would have videoed it all on my phone."

I frowned, and my cat let out a little growl. "No, you can't film any of it," I said. And Mr. Mittens nodded.

"I wouldn't have shown anyone," she whined. "It doesn't matter, anyway. I was too busy holding onto the tree and trying to wish the unicorn away."

Hmpf. Mr. Mittens shook himself, and when he stopped, he was in his Ragdoll shape. He started to walk away, looking back at us, and encouraged us to follow. We looked at each other and followed him. Of course, he was my protector. I should never have brought my human friend into these woods without him. A wave of gratitude washed over me, and I sent a thought full of love and thankfulness to him. His tail shot up, and the tip flipped back and forth in his kitty acknowledgment.

He led us to the former clearing we'd been searching for. It wasn't that far away, and frankly, we'd probably walked through it a couple of times without recognition.

Mr. Mittens stopped, his tail swished a few times, then he sat and looked at me. *The altar is here.*

"Thank you."

My cat was rarely curious about me, so I was surprised when he asked me why I needed to come back here.

"I'm going to summon my great-grandfather. Your friend."

His eyes opened wider. *Why?*

That caused me to doubt my reasoning again. But I couldn't see another path.

"I need to know about my magic to help Gabe and to just *know.* I don't have anyone else to ask."

He looked thoughtful. *Hmpf. I'm not sure summoning a Fae lord is a good idea.*

"Why not? He's my family."

The Fae are not as you are.

"How so?"

They are less emotional. More driven by duty and honor. Your grandfather may not be happy that you summoned him. He could punish you.

I second guessed myself again, worried I was putting the three of us in unnecessary danger. But he was family, and I had no other options.

"Did he punish his wife? His daughter?" I argued.

They did not summon him when I knew him.

My thoughts were dark. I didn't have a choice. I couldn't see another answer. To save Gabe, I had to know my abilities. I couldn't face a witch with power equal to mine. She'd lived her whole life knowing her limits, using her magic, and understanding it.

"I don't see a choice," I said, finally.

He acknowledged my decision with a swish of his tail. Then, I reached for my earth magic, seeking the altar deep in the ground. Once I sensed it, I ordered it to rise again. The earth slipped around the stone altar and lifted it almost as though it were floating to the top.

Once above ground, I straightened it and cleaned it with a thought. Then, since we'd need the space, I ordered the greenery around it for twelve feet to return to the ground, and it did. Finally, the altar sat on a small clear patch of earth.

"Well, there's the altar," I said. "We can't wait for a full moon, since we just had one, and I'm not waiting a month to save Gabe. Plus, I doubt that's really important. It will just have to be a waning gibbous. However, we should still do it at the moon's zenith."

Megan nodded along with my commentary.

"I think your magic will make up for the moon," she said.

I guessed I'd impressed her.

"Let's hope."

Or not hope, if what Mr. Mittens said was true. If I were snatched from my realm, I'd probably be grumpy, too. I took a deep breath and let it out slowly. I wasn't up for this. I just wanted to sleep and heal, but I couldn't leave Gabe in this mess. He'd just been helping me. It wasn't fair to him. I strengthened my resolve, and the three of us headed back to the house to prepare for tonight and the not so full moon.

Chapter Four

I put all the supplies we'd gathered into a bag. Megan was going to carry it, since I was hurting a whole lot worse by nightfall. Unfortunately, the moon wasn't going to hit its zenith until 3:23 a.m. The witching hour indeed. I giggled.

We tried to sleep some, but we were too wound up or scared for that to happen, so we just lay in my bed and talked like schoolgirls at a sleepover until it was time to leave. Mr. Mittens escorted us to the altar. Megan was excited to see more magic and a real fairy. But I was terrified. If Gabe's life and independence weren't at stake, I'd bail on this endeavor. I knew some magic. I could get by. But I couldn't bail on him. I cared about him. Also, I knew how he felt about being controlled by witches, I couldn't let that go.

Megan held the lantern so I could read the symbols and copy them onto the altar. I'd practiced the movements earlier, and I did again so when the time came, I'd be ready. Even though the night was cool and a breeze drifted through the trees, I was sweating. What if this didn't work? I didn't have a backup plan to save Gabe. I'd just have to go after Sofia directly, but I'd probably lose. What if it did work? From what I'd read in fiction, the Fae were fickle and alien. This could be worse than attacking Sofia directly. I shivered. What if I conjured the wrong Fae? How would I know? The bad outweighed the good. I just had to trust that by using my blood, he'd be the one summoned. My great-grandmother just got lucky.

The moon cleared the trees and beamed down on us. Its cool light touched me with a physical weight. The comforting, cool magic enveloped me, and I knew it was time. I used my pocketknife and pricked my finger with the sharp blade tip. I let three drops fall onto the altar. I did the initial movements, although I felt silly dancing around the altar. Plus, it hurt. A lot. Megan held the light over the book, and I read the spell, pushing my magic into it and completing the final arm movements before the altar.

"Come to me, fair one. Help me with this task. See me, obey me. Grant me what I ask." With all my might and the magic he'd given me, I willed that my great-grandfather would appear.

I stepped back from the altar. I grabbed Megan's hand and held on tightly. The glacial moon bathed the altar with its cold light. I was trembling, terrified. Nothing happened.

Megan and I looked at each other. "Did I say something wrong?" I asked her.

She shrugged. "Nope. That spell was simple."

"What about the movements?"

"You did everything that the book said, perfectly. The spell is just stupid."

"Yeah, and she was a wi—"

BANG

A blast of light and sound hit us with the force of a

truck. We flew off our feet and bounced on our hind ends painfully.

Megan groaned. I was groaning. All of my pain sensors screamed.

"Who dares to summon me!" A voice rumbled through the forest. A bright halo of light surrounded the figure.

I stood and brushed the dirt off my backside. Then, not knowing what else to do, I raised my hand. "I did."

The figure frowned.

I had no idea what I expected my grandfather to look like. Both my great-grandmother and my grandmother had said he was handsome. So, I'd pictured him like Legolas from the *Lord of the Rings* movies. Long flowing blonde hair, perfect, glowing skin, with a lithe figure dressed like Robin Hood with a bow in his hand. Graceful and poised in all he did, and perfect, pointed little ears peeking through his hair. I was *extremely* wrong.

The figure before us was domineering. That was the only word for it. He was tall and powerful and looked more like a Viking than a lithe elf. His hair was short and dark red. His grey eyes blazed with fury. Hard leather armor over some silvery chainmail covered his body. His shield was slung over his back, and in addition to the ax in his hands, a sword was strapped at his waist. If he didn't look like he was going to kill us with the ginormous ax in his hands, I'd have called him handsome.

"Hello, great-grandfather," I choked out, my voice squeaky and unsure in front of this monster of a man. Where were the pointy ears? This must be like a unicorn. Total propaganda. Little people with wings, my eye.

"Who are you?" the voice boomed.

"Umm, I'm Brigid. The great-granddaughter of Niamh, granddaughter of Lucy Rose, daughter of Aiden."

His frown deepened. "What do you want of me, child?"

"This is a long story; do you want to come to the house for some tea?" I asked politely. Megan was still on the ground, trying to look small and disappear behind me.

"I was preparing for battle. I cannot stay."

"Well, I've just had a battle with a coven of witches. They are stealing my magic, and they've taken my boyfriend. That's why I need you. My family is dead. I didn't know about magic, and I have to learn fast. You're all I have left."

He contemplated me, taking in the bruises and swelling in my face, and the painful way I stood.

"I will come for…" He looked like the word was distasteful. "Tea."

"Thank you, grandfather."

He put the ax in a holder on his belt. I wondered if all that metal pulled his pants down if he wasn't holding on to it, but the belt was hefty and looked tight. Probably part of why he was grumpy. I gritted my teeth and pulled Megan up. Mr. Mittens had stayed out of the way, but now he led the way back, his glowing fur lighting the path.

I opened the door for my grandfather, and we followed him in. I turned the kettle on. He sat at the table and crossed his massive arms over his equally massive chest. I was not going to believe a single fantasy story ever again.

Mr. Mittens stared at my grandfather. Eventually, they nodded at each other. Maybe Mr. Mittens and my grandfather had been communicating. I'd ask the cat later. Mr. Mittens leapt up on the counter, out of the way, but didn't leave. Megan sat as far from my grandfather as she could. I sat next to him.

"This is my friend Megan, she is helping me," I started the conversation.

My grandfather sneered. "She is human."

"Yes, so? She's a good friend."

He looked at me. "I cannot teach you all about magic in the few hours I can spare. What is it you want from me?"

His attitude was understandable but wearing on me. I needed him, he was family, and I shouldn't have to beg for his help. I was growing increasingly irritated.

"Look, gramps, I have had a whole magical heritage hidden from me, I have witches breathing down my neck, I can't get this house finished, and I have to free my possible soulmate from the evilest bitch I've ever known. I need to know how to free someone from a witch's control. And I need it without the attitude and the intimidation." I must have really lost it. I was standing and leaning over the table and in his face. I had no idea what had come over me.

He smiled, but it wasn't a warm smile. "You have spirit, child of mine."

"Thanks." I sat back down.

"You may call me Lugh."

"Is that your name?" I knew enough about the Fae that I doubted he'd give me his name.

"It is near enough."

I nodded. Just what I thought. His name hadn't been written in any of the journals, only that he was a Fae lord. I didn't really know what that meant, but if they lived in a feudal system, probably someone with some power that reported to a king.

"Can you help me with this witch problem?"

"I cannot remain in your realm for long. I have responsibilities I must not shirk. And this place drains my power and makes me weak. Your training may be long and would best take place on my land in my realm. However, I can help you free your mate."

"Really? How?"

He stood and reached out. I leaned back, away from him. He took back his hand. He sighed. "I need to touch you to give you the knowledge you require."

I gave him a sheepish smile. "Sorry. I don't like to be touched." I leaned back in.

He placed his hand on my head and closed his eyes. Megan was quiet, but drinking it all in, her eyes flicking between us. Mr. Mittens was curled up on the counter. He looked relaxed, but I was more attuned to him, and every cell of his Ragdoll self was focused on us. He didn't appear alarmed, so I also shut my eyes.

The magic hit me like a bomb. Fire raced from my head to my toes. I might have cried out. But then knowledge on how to break a witch's spell surged through my synapses. I panted with the pain of it all.

"That should be what you need," Lugh said. "Knowledge absorbed this way is painful. It will require time to settle in and be sure in your mind. Sleep, child. You will know what to do when you awaken."

"Thank you, grandfather," I choked out. My head pounded with the beat of my heart. This was worse than a migraine. I blinked at him.

"I will contact you about training your magic," he said.

The kettle whistled. I grabbed my head as the sound sent a spike of agony through it. Megan stood and shut off the burner.

"I'll make your tea," I said to my grandfather and stood to do so.

His eyes flicked up to the left, as though he'd heard a summons. "I must go."

Before I could say anything else, a blinding light exploded around him, and he vanished. I gasped at the additional pain the light caused. I sat down heavily, holding my head in my hands.

"Let's put you to bed," Megan said.

I waved my hand to acknowledge her, but I couldn't speak. She helped me up and guided me to the bedroom. I couldn't see, the pain was so severe. She tucked me in, and I fell asleep quickly, my mind and body overwhelmed by my grandfather's gift.

Chapter Five

I woke up late. The headache was gone, and I knew how to break the witch's spell. Megan was already up, I could hear dishes banging and smell food, so she must be cooking breakfast. I stretched and got up.

Megan looked at me oddly when I came in. I was smiling, so that might have been why.

"Your bruises are gone," she said.

I reached up and felt my face. All the swelling was gone, and I noticed I had no other pain. I started to laugh.

"Why are you laughing?"

"My grandfather must have healed me, and I can break the spell on Gabe," I said smugly.

"OK. Can you stop the witch? Can you get your magic back from her?"

I frowned; she was killing my mood. "No."

"I didn't mean to ruin your day, but until we have a plan, are you sure we should break the spell on your Gabe?"

I sat at the table and drank the coffee sitting in front of me. Should I break the spell? I thought for a moment.

Remembering back to what Gabe had told me about his marriage and the previous encounters he'd had with witch covens, I had only one decision to make.

"Yes, we need to break the spell. Then, he can decide what he wants. We can't leave him without the opportunity to make his own choice."

After that, I felt a wave of relief wash over me. I took a breath and let it out. Then we ate. As soon as Gabe was home from work, we had a witch's spell to break.

———

Just like before, we pulled behind Gabe's house and knocked on the door. He answered. No sign of recognition lit his eyes. We were strangers, again. I sighed. Oh well. As long as he kept the door open for a minute, I could do this thing. Megan and I had discussed a plan to keep him busy while I worked the magic I needed to.

She babbled on with some story she concocted on the fly about being lost and trying to meet someone secretly and blah, blah, blah. Meanwhile I gathered my will and reached out to the spell resting on Gabe's mind. Just as she was coming to the end with "...so can you tell us where that is?" I pushed with my magic, and the spell snapped. At least that is what it felt like to me—an inaudible snap like a rubber band pulled back and released quickly. Megan's amulet flashed at the same time, and she reached up to grab it. Gabe wobbled back a few steps and blinked several times. Then, he stood up straight.

"Brigid?"

"I'm here."

He looked disoriented. I'm sure he was. I thought he'd

ask me what had happened, but his countenance turned dark and angry.

"Come in, we don't have very long."

We both walked in, and he closed the door. We sat on his sofa.

"Sofia will be here at six thirty," he said. "She has to come every day and 'freshen up' her spell on me. By evening, I have terrible headaches. I've been fighting against the compulsion she keeps on me, the block against my freedom."

"Gabe, I'm so sorry. I didn't know how to free you before."

He crossed the room from the chair he was in, to the sofa, and pulled me up. He wrapped me in a hug and held me tight, his face buried in my hair. "I knew you'd find a way. That hope was trapped in my heart under her spell. I may not have remembered you, but somewhere, deep inside I knew you'd come."

Emotion grabbed my heart and squeezed until it was hard to breathe. It took all I had not to cry at his confession.

"Thanks, Bridge," he said softly.

He released me, and I smiled up at him. "Always."

"She'll come and put the spell back on me," he said.

I nodded my head. "That's why you should come with us."

He shook his head. "I don't know if I can. She'll find out, and it'll be worse for you."

"Gabe, I'm so sorry. If you hadn't helped me, this wouldn't have happened to you."

He shook his head. "She'd have found a way. This was always her plan. Don't fool yourself." He walked us back to the door.

Megan walked ahead. He leaned down and kissed me.

"You, it's always been you I've wanted. No matter what she says, don't forget that," he said ominously.

A wave of nausea overwhelmed me. He'd called Sofia his girlfriend before. What else had she made him do?

He noticed my face had gone pale. "Come by in two days. She's going out of town. You can unwhammy me, and we'll plan our next steps." Then he kissed me again and closed the door.

I had many questions. If she had to "whammy" him daily, how could she leave for two days? What other kind of nasty thing was she setting up? I understood his reasons for remaining behind—he was protecting me. That broke my heart. I knew how much he hated being controlled.

As we cleared his street and pulled out on the highway, we passed Sofia. She looked directly at me. I felt ill. Did she know I'd been at Gabe's? Was she going to do something more to hurt him because I'd been to see him? Should we turn around and take him with us? No. I had to trust he knew what was best, but I cried all the way home, knowing I'd made the wrong choice. Megan desperately tried to comfort me.

When we returned, Mr. Mittens was waiting for us on the railing of the back porch.

Your grandfather has sent you a gift, he said. His mental voice was off, uncertain.

My crying jag had drained me, as had leaving Gabe to the sadistic wiles of the bitch witch queen. My curiosity barely piqued.

"Oh?" I said. Not completely engaged in his agitated body language.

I went to open the door.

You may want to walk in slowly, my cat said. That gave me pause.

This time I was curious. "Why?" I asked pointedly. It was my house after all.

He sent your magic teacher.

"Oh, that's nice," I answered. I twisted the knob to enter.

I took one look inside, then backed out and shut the door.

"Mr. Mittens, what is sitting at my kitchen table?"

He licked a paw, attempting to be nonchalant, but I could tell he was also shaken by the thing my grandfather had sent to teach me. *That is a Kelpie.*

"A Kelpie," I repeated. From what I remembered from high school English class, a Kelpie was a water horse—a creature that enticed humans into the water and drowned them. Why would my grandfather send such a thing to me? He'd healed me, and helped me, surely he wasn't trying to kill me?

She is technically only half Kelpie. The other half is Fae, Mr. Mittens corrected. *She's your great grandfather's mistress of magic.*

"My life is strange," I mumbled.

Megan's face lit up. "It might be, but it's sure a lot more interesting than before!"

I gave her a sidelong glance. "That's the understatement of the year."

I had to save Gabe. To do that, I had to learn magic— apparently from a Kelpie, a Scottish-Fae monster.

I'd thought that to accomplish my goal, I'd learn some-thing quick and be done. I needed this to help Gabe. I hoped he could hold on. I sighed and opened the door to face my fate at the hands of my teacher.

"Hi, I'm Brigid."

The half Fae looked up at me. She'd obviously made herself at home; she had a cup of tea in her hand and a pastry. I didn't even know I had pastries. The Kelpie had long curly green hair and a faint greenish tinge to her skin. She had the pointed ears, go figure, but they were distinctly horsey—long, pointed, and on top of her head—they flicked around with any sound. Her hands had long fingers, six of them on each hand, and long claws. I wondered how she held such a delicate cup with those things. Her lashes were long, but they covered eyes, which were as black as night, and there was no white sclera at the edges. She could not pass as remotely human.

She looked up at me, unimpressed. She nodded her head in a slight bow of acknowledgement. "You can call me Dana." She had a thick accent I couldn't place. There was a burr and a lilt to it like a cross somewhere between Scottish and Irish, although I wasn't any kind of expert.

"Umm," I said, uncertain where to start. "Mr. Mittens said my grandfather sent you?"

The Kelpie nodded. "He did."

I waited for more information, but none was forthcoming. I had the distinct feeling that not only was Dana not impressed with me, but she wasn't very happy to be here.

"I'm happy you took time out of your life to help me learn magic," I prompted.

Her shark eyes bore into me. "I'm not here out of a sense of magnanimity. I was ordered here by my lord. We aren't going to be friends, and I expect you to do exactly as I say when I say it."

I looked at her for a moment. I didn't have time for this. Yes, I needed to learn magic yesterday, but I couldn't be locked down while I did it. I had werewolves to talk to, a boyfriend to free, a house to finish, and a business to get off the ground. I couldn't spend twenty-four seven being a slave to a creepy magic teacher.

Instead of accepting her terms, I asked. "What will this entail?" Megan gasped slightly behind me.

The Kelpie finished the last bite of her pastry and licked her fingers. Her green tongue was long and pointed. Yuck.

"While we practice, you will obey."

"How long each day will it take?"

"It depends on how quickly you learn."

I sighed. "OK."

My new teacher looked smug. She stood and clip-clopped to the door behind me. I realized that her feet were horse's hooves. She was clad in an ivory silk robe, and I wondered briefly if she had a horse tail as well.

She threw all three of us a disdainful glance and said, "We'll start at dawn." Then in a golden flash, she vanished.

Chapter Six

"Mr. Mittens!" I bellowed after the Kelpie's dramatic exit.

Yes, he sighed. As he strolled in the door left open by the Kelpie.

"What did my grandfather say to you?" I demanded. Obviously, they'd spoken more about me than I'd thought the evening before.

We discussed you, of course. I'm your protector.

"That's not gonna fly this time. Explain to me what that means, and what you and he discussed, *exactly*." My hands were on my hips, and I stared down at him.

His face seemed to become grumpier before my eyes, which wasn't an easy feat. He always looked a little grouchy.

Well, he began. His eyes shifted to the door.

He'd better not be planning to escape.

Megan and I leaned in to hear what he was going to say, even though it was in our heads. My cat could work a room.

I just explained to him how much you were struggling with magic without anyone to teach you, he finally admitted.

I looked at him a minute longer before speaking. I

wasn't sure I believed him. He probably made me out to be much more pathetic than I was, but I couldn't read his cute kitty face, and he was sitting on his fluffy tail so that couldn't give himself away.

"Hmmm, are you sure that's all?"

He blinked, the picture of innocence, and then was silent. He wasn't an idiot. He knew I'd catch him in a lie if he kept talking.

I doubted my patheticness would be enough to convince my great-grandfather to send me his "mistress of magic," so I knew that Mr. Mittens had told him something else, something important. I could be wrong, maybe I'd guilted him into helping me, but you never knew.

"So, I need to know about this Dana. What do you know about her?"

She's powerful and terrifying. She'll hate you for taking her away from her duties, which include torture and finding new ways to break your grandfather's enemies through magic. He looked away again.

I was starting to think he wasn't looking for an escape but looking for danger. "What's the matter? Why do you keep looking at the door?"

I'm sensing an incursion. I must go.

He walked to the door and looked at me, so I knew to open it for him. "Fine, but remember, ask before you kill."

He raced out, and I shut the door. Megan looked at me strangely when I turned back around. "What did that mean?"

I sighed. "He thinks something dangerous, think unicorn, has popped up on my property."

She rolled her eyes. "I know what he meant. What did you mean by 'ask before you kill'?"

"Oh, when I first met Brightfeather, he was trying to kill her. I stopped him. After talking to her, we realized she was only here for sanctuary, not to kill me," I answered distractedly. My mind was already on the list of things I needed to do before I met with Dana in the morning.

"Okaaay."

"Yeah, I love my cat, but he thinks he's badass."

"He is. You saw him take out the horned pony from hell."

"Yeah, I guess he is."

"You're distracted, what's going on in your head?"

I shrugged. "I need to contact the werewolves and let them know what's going on. We're working together on the witch problem. Their dad was fond of Gabe, too."

She nodded. "OK, call them."

I looked at the clock. "You don't think it's too late, do you?"

She gave me a hard look. "It's seven thirty. You're avoiding it."

I was. I was nervous since it had taken me so long to recover. I didn't want them to think that I wasn't pulling my weight after they'd fought so hard against the coven. I was a pathetic ally. "No, I'm calling now."

I pulled out my phone and dialed Luke. He answered after two rings, so I knew he was anxious.

"Hi, Luke. It's Brigid."

"Brigid! I've been worried about you. Are you feeling any better?" At that, all my worry melted away. It'd been a stupid thing, mostly a leftover from years of emotional abuse. He didn't think I was worthless, just hurt.

"Much better. Thanks so much! It really helped that my friend came out to help me."

"That's nice. What a good friend."

I looked at Megan. She really was a good friend. I smiled at her. Luke was also a good friend. He'd taken the time to ask about me even though I'm sure he was anxious about what I'd discovered.

"I saw Gabe. He's physically well," I started the conversation.

"Yeah, we checked at the clinic," Luke responded. "Brigid, how would you feel if we met quickly? That way everyone can hear what you have to say."

I looked at Megan. I wasn't sure how she'd like being bombarded by a family full of werewolves. I hit the mute on my phone. "Would you be OK if the wolves came over?"

She looked a little intimidated, but said, "Sure, if they're as good looking as you promised."

I rolled my eyes, then I unmuted. "Do you want to come here?"

"Sure, have you and your friend eaten? Does she know?"

"Yeah, she knows everything, we can talk freely. No, we haven't eaten."

"We'll bring pizza. See you in an hour." He hung up. I looked down at the phone with a frown. He hadn't even ended with a goodbye. Oh well. He must be busy.

"They'll be here in an hour," I said to Megan.

"Good grief," she replied and ran upstairs to fix herself up.

I went to my bathroom to wash my face. Hopefully the swelling in my eyes from crying would go down before anyone saw me.

To my surprise, the entire Whelan clan showed up with several pizzas. They weren't the entire pack. I'd learned from Luke earlier, there were several other families that completed it, but they were the leaders. I introduced Megan to everyone, and I could tell she was smitten with both Noah, the new alpha, and Lucas, the second oldest brother. The other Whelans, Anna, the mother, Michael the third, and the two sisters, Isabella and Madison, made up the rest of the party. Anna was one of those timeless, handsome women, and her daughters took after her with their blonde hair and green eyes. The boys had varying shades of blonde hair from dirty blond to dark honey blond on Luke. But all of their eyes were the clear, bright shade of green like their mother's.

Luckily, my table could hold eight people, if I brought back the extra chairs I had doing extra duty around the house. The two eldest Whelan brothers weren't that tall, probably in the average range, but they were physically intimidating. They were strong and broad shouldered. Michael, the youngest, was slightly taller and leaner. The girls and their mother were all shapely, but not that imposing physically. It was strange to think that this family of normal looking people could transform into terrifying wolves, twice the size of normal ones. If I hadn't seen it myself, I'd never believe it.

Once everyone had food and was eating around the table, Noah started. "Thanks for having us over, Brigid, we're happy to see you looking so much better. Is this." He waved at my face. "Because of Gabe?"

I shook my head until I swallowed the bite in my mouth. "No. I saw him, but he doesn't remember me."

They all stopped and looked up, my newly healed form, forgotten.

"What do you mean?" Isabella said.

"When I saw him, he knew exactly who I was," Noah added with a frown. He was the serious one of the family.

"She doesn't want him to remember her," Megan said with around a mouthful of pizza.

They all looked at her. She shut her mouth and looked abashed.

"It's true. We saw him twice. The first time he couldn't remember me at all, or his car that we returned. When he almost broke through, he had a terrible headache and told us to leave. The second time, I broke the spell on him. He told us that she was keeping him in a controlled state that she had to renew nightly," I said.

I was growing more and more upset and stopped before I started crying again. I took a bite of my pizza, even though it tasted like ash, to hide my growing emotions.

Megan noticed, as did Anna. While Megan filled in the rest of the story, Anna patted my hand comfortingly. I felt guilt rise up to join my other churning emotions—she had just lost her husband. I should be comforting her. That gave me the boost I needed to shove down the emotions and answer the questions everyone had.

"So, why is Sofia leaving him for two days? That sounds rather convenient if she's having to renew her spell every night," Luke said.

We hadn't had time to question Gabe; he'd shooed us out too quickly. It had been eating at me as well, so I figured it was best to see if anyone else had a possible explanation. My gut was saying she'd concocted something nasty in place of her spell.

"We don't know," I answered for me and Megan. "But I have a bad feeling. What do you all think?"

The werewolves looked perplexed and muttered some things to each other. Finally, Noah spoke up. "She's got something up her sleeve. So far, she's out planned us. If she's leaving him alone, she's going to do something to keep us away and to keep him from coming to us."

That was exactly what my gut was saying, so I agreed. "What do we do about it?"

Noah looked around at his family. "We'll be there. We'll set up a watch around his property and attempt to keep him safe." He gestured at Isabella. "Izzy will follow him to work and home."

My heart rate accelerated. I was causing them to take time from their lives. "What about your jobs?" I asked. "I'm free, and so is Megan, we can follow instead."

Noah shook his head. "No, we both saw how badly you were injured, and Megan is human. The witch and her coven would chew her up. We're werewolves. We may not have active magic, but we're tough. Plus, Sofia already knows you, and who knows how she'll react if she sees you around Gabriel."

Isabella chimed in, "I'm free right now—we're in between jobs. We've got the time, don't worry."

I accepted their reasoning, but I still felt bad. Their husband and father had been killed so the witches could steal my magic. Yet, the Whelans were still loyal to me and willing to help. I didn't deserve their friendship and kindness.

"I know I'm the lone human, but Sofia doesn't know me. I'm a total stranger. Wouldn't it make sense that I'm involved?" Megan asked.

Everyone looked at her. I was afraid. She was my best friend, and other than the protection in her charm, totally defenseless against a witch. But she was right, and looking at all the faces around me, the wolves agreed. They'd been trying to keep her out, but it made too much sense to not involve her.

Noah gave a terse nod. As the new alpha, they all looked at him, and that was that.

"She can go with me. That way, she can drive, I can go wolf, and we'll cover all the bases," Isabella said.

"That'll be great," Megan confirmed, but her face was a shade paler, and I knew she was scared.

"OK, we've got a plan." Noah sighed. "I think we also have a complete list of the coven members."

I stiffened. That was good news. "Yes?" I prompted after a moment. Then because it had been weighing on me I asked, "What are they saying about the dead members? I haven't heard anything about missing people in the local news."

Madison answered. "My job was to find out that particular information. Apparently, they've gone on a two week-long 'retreat.' I'm guessing something will go horribly wrong to explain why they don't come back."

"Yeah, like they messed with the wrong werewolf pack." I heard Luke comment under his breath. The Whelans were definitely as angry at the coven as I was.

"I'm so sorry," I blurted out. "I didn't know this would happen when you came to work for me. I'd give anything to bring him back."

Anna's eyes filled with tears. She wiped them away unselfconsciously and reached over to grip my hand. "Don't go there, dear. It was not your fault. It was the witches, and don't you forget that. Not one of us"—she looked around at her family—"and I mean no one in this family blames you."

I stood, leaned over, and hugged her. She returned the hug. I sat back in my chair. "Thank you. You don't know how much that means to me."

They all nodded, faces full of love and care, and I believed them.

"I'll email you the list we've compiled," Noah said. "They are in just about every business in this town," he added, ominously.

My stomach churned, and I wondered if I'd be able to hold down my supper.

They finished the pizza and sat around chatting about anything else except for witches and magic. I noticed that Luke and Megan had hit it off. They were talking quietly in the corner of the kitchen, he was leaning with his back against part of the counter, Megan was leaning on the opposing one, and they were oblivious to the rest of us. I smiled. Izzy, after Noah had called her that I couldn't think of her any other way, pulled me aside for a moment.

"They look cozy."

I looked over at Megan again and smiled. "Yeah."

"Luke had a bad breakup a year ago, and this is the first time I've seen him even look at another girl." She sipped her drink and watched them. They remained oblivious.

I nodded. I didn't know what to say to that. Megan was a good, dependable soul, and he could do a lot worse.

"Yeah, she was upset because he 'kept secrets' from her. Her words. It was the werewolf thing. It's agreed in the magical world that humans must remain ignorant."

Was she telling me that because I broke a rule? I must have blanched because she placed a hand on my arm.

"Don't worry, we don't have a police force." She smirked. "I was telling you that because that's already a barrier gone for them, if this"—she gestured at them—"goes further." She paused and sipped her soda. "I'm happy, Brigid. Don't worry. I won't let him hurt your friend. He's a good man, too."

I already knew that. Of all the Whelans, I felt closest to Luke. We'd been the ones that had spoken the most about the house, and I'd been with him when his dad died. Craig, the Whelans' dad, was the perfect example of a great family man. He loved and cared for his family so much. Just looking at them now, all close and loving, was enough to let me know that Luke had a great example. He'd be a great boyfriend, or more. I'd feel good about it if he and Megan chose each other. Of course, this was their first meeting, so both Izzy and I were probably far ahead of the game, but it filled me with warmth that we were both hoping for them to get together.

"I didn't come over here for that, I just want to reassure you that I'll look after her."

I shrugged. "I know you will." I smiled at her. "You Whelans are good people."

"Are you sure? We can be ravening beasts."

She looked so sincere at that, that my face must have shown the surprise I felt.

She laughed. "Don't worry, we can control it, but your face! Priceless."

I realized she was joking around with me. Since previous to this, we'd only worked professionally, and Isabella was *very* professional, I laughed, too. Maybe I'd made a new friend to replace the one I'd lost.

"Izzy, do any of your pack know anything about Kelpies?"

She blinked at me. "Uh, I don't, but I'll ask. Are Kelpies something we need to worry about along with witches?"

"No." I laughed and shook my head. "That seems to be a particular problem of mine."

Chapter Seven

My alarm went off before it was light. I wanted to be dressed, ready, and full of warm food and coffee before my strange teacher arrived. Megan was sleeping in, and I was careful not to disturb her. I was nervous, and truth be told, a little terrified.

I was finishing up my coffee, when Mr. Mittens licked the last morsel from his bowl and looked up, so I was prepared when a flash of light announced her arrival.

Her imperious expression froze when she saw him. Then to my surprise, she gave a stiff little bow in his direction. "Xrsrphn," she greeted him.

He returned the bow with a slight dip of his head. "Mistress Dana."

I raised a questioning eyebrow at him, and intoned, "Xrsrphn?"

It's my true name.

I wanted to ask him why he hadn't shared his true name with me, but before I could, my new magic teacher cracked her whip.

"Xrsrphn, you will guide us to the place of power," she commanded.

Place of power? What was she talking about? My eyes were on my cat. Only the swish of his tail betrayed his annoyance at her demand. But he led us out the kitchen door, down the porch steps, and across the gravel drive to the waterfall trail.

I followed behind my new teacher, apprehension tight in my throat. We passed the place where I'd run into a black bear and her cubs, passed the spring, and continued towards the waterfall. Is that where we were going for sure?

I pushed a question out from my mind to his, *Is the water-fall a place of power?*

It is. This is why your grandmother hid the trail.

How much power are we talking about, and what kind of power?

But instead of an answer, I got his usual annoyed *Hmpf.*

We marched along a little further. I kept my eyes on him because I could feel his anxiety. I couldn't figure out what it was about. He was obviously acquainted with Dana; he didn't seem afraid of her. I understood a moment later, when he stopped in the middle of the trail and faced us.

I must leave you here. There is an incursion. He looked at Dana. *Brigid will lead you to the place of power.* With that, he twisted into his Splintercat form and bounded away.

I sighed. I wasn't comfortable with my magic teacher. I'd been hoping his solid presence would be with me. That's the real reason he'd been tense not the incursion. He didn't want to leave me alone with her either.

The Kelpie frowned but motioned for me to take the lead. I took her up to the waterfall. I hated having her in my personal sanctuary. I'd always been most at peace in this location. The thrum of the water, the way the sun always seemed to shine on my favorite boulder perch, the smell of the rhododendrons and evergreens always whispered "home" to me. I stopped at the edge of the small pool and looked at her expectantly.

A small creeping trickle of fear trailed down my spine as I realized I'd brought a water horse to a pond. But I pushed it down. Surely, my grandfather wouldn't send her here only to kill me. He'd been helpful.

"Let me see what you have learned so far," the Kelpie said. "This is the heart of your power; you'll have the most control and strength here. Amaze me."

Great, a snarky Kelpie who hated me. At least she hadn't attempted to kill me yet.

Since I'd practiced here many times, I figured I'd start with water. I turned to the pond and coaxed a stream of water to rise from the pond. I sent it in a swirl, and it rose and gamboled through the air. Then I formed it into the shape of a butterfly and made it beat its wings in a circle before I released it back to the pond. I was best with water, and I smiled at my perfect display of control. I looked at Dana, she gestured that I should continue. No praise, no criticism—tough crowd.

OK, next. Fire. I looked around. There was a bunch of tree litter on my favorite rock. I silently directed the fire in me to consume it. When it lit up, I ordered the fire to form a flower, and then I let it burn out, cleansing the stone. I was proud of myself, that fire flower was a perfect replica of a rhododendron bloom. Before my teacher could demand more, I confidently instructed the earth around my boulder to burst into wildflowers. Then, I commanded a single bolt of lightning down from the sky. It hit the water, which splashed and boiled and sprayed us with water. I grimaced. I hadn't intended to get us wet. I glanced at my teacher briefly to gauge her mood.

She still frowned at me. I had no way to show her mind magic or spirit. In fact, I barely understood those aspects of my power. I'd lost ice, I'd never done anything with shadow, and I obviously had little control of lightning. The last one was light. I hadn't practiced that one much, but I funneled the light from the sun to come down and twinkle in a ball in my hand. I tossed it up, caught it and dispersed it. When I was done, I looked at my teacher—hopeful she'd find that I wasn't a complete loser.

"That's all?" she intoned, and my stomach sank. I was a failure.

"Yes?" I squeaked.

"Is that a question? Don't you know?" she asked with an imperious tone.

I didn't trust my voice, so I stood there and waited for more judgement to land like blows.

"My master was right, you are wholly ignorant and unprepared," she muttered to herself. "Pathetic," she spoke directly to me.

I sighed. I already knew that. The witches had kicked my butt less than a week ago. I had power. I knew that. But using it? Just like she said, pathetic. The little bit of confidence I'd pulled from fled.

"We have a lot of work. The only magic you seem almost competent at are water, fire, and earth. So, we'll start there to at least raise you to competency at something."

It looked like a long road ahead.

"First, what are you using to focus your energy?"

Focus my energy? I'd only been using my mind and will. I didn't know I was supposed to use anything else.

"Umm, nothing?"

"No wonder. For you to advance, you need to start small and precise. A focusing object would be best." She looked at

73

me and tapped one of her horse hooves against a stone. "Do you wear any jewelry consistently?"

I looked down to the spot my wedding ring used to be. I'd tossed that over a bridge in a fit of pique during the divorce. It was dumb, but it made me feel good. I'd begged my husband earlier in our marriage to replace it after we'd had monetary success, but he'd ignored me. One of the many red flags I'd ignored throughout our marriage.

I shook my head. "No, but I was used to wearing a ring. I can start again." My grandmother had left me a lot of jewelry. I'd pick something I liked with *good* memories.

"Fine, we'll start there. Call the ring to you."

"What?"

This time my teacher sighed. "Your ignorance is daunting. You are Fae. It should be part of your inherent magic. Call the object."

I didn't want to be called any more names, so I pictured my jewelry box, and focused on grandmother's engagement ring. It was a pretty thing. Art déco. A classic cut diamond surrounded by filigree. I'd assumed it was white gold, but now? Maybe it was silver. She was part Fae as I was, and the Fae had an affinity to silver. I pictured the ring firmly in my head and called it to me.

I remembered that Mr. Mittens had told me once I could call anything. But there were rules. It had to exist, and I had to be careful in case it was ripped from someone who didn't believe in magic. This exercise meant I was safe from exposing magic.

I opened my hand so the ring would have a landing spot. Nothing. Great, one more thing for my teacher to complain about. Just as I was about to try again, something flashed by my face and tinkled as it landed on my favorite boulder. I looked at the rock. Sure enough, the ring lay there twinkling in the sun. I grinned. I wasn't a complete magical disaster. I slipped the ring on.

"Hmmm. That was adequate," Dana remarked. "Now, you will call a single drop of water. Focus through the ring. Concentrate on it and lift a single drop from the waterfall."

Great. I could sometimes do small magics, but I'd never done anything that small. We were probably about to get drenched. I focused through the ring, as she'd directed me. That was an odd feeling. I was used to looking at what I did, but now I had to rely on my will and imagination. I reached out and called a drop of water to me. My magic reacted—a coolness in my chest that I associated with my water magic. I lifted the water. My eyes flicked to it. Sure enough, not a drop, more like a cup. She frowned. I released the water, and it splashed back into the pool. I tried to keep my thoughts positive, but Evan's voice echoed between my ears that I would never be good at this. I shook my head. He was wrong. I'd already accomplished so much. I could do it, I just needed practice and instruction. I kept at it. Plus, I did not want to disappoint Dana or more importantly my great-grandfather. For one, I wasn't sure she wouldn't just drown me in my own pond. Kelpies had that reputation.

It took a couple of hours, but I was finally able to call one drop of water consistently. Once I was pronounced "adequate," she left in her usual blaze of light, promising more delights tomorrow. My magic usually exhilarated me and left me full of energy, but today? I was drained. My mental facilities hadn't been strained like that in a long time. I'd exhausted myself fighting my self-doubt, and I'd taxed my concentration. I dragged myself down the trail, forgetting to call my cat.

As I strolled down the path, mind elsewhere, I was stopped by a snake. I knew that there were snakes in

Oregon, although I'd never seen many here. We'd had rattlers in Utah, so I was cautious near snakes, but not really worried about them. However, before I just skipped around it, my mind finally caught up to me, and I realized it was bright red. That registered as *not* normal.

I stopped and studied the creature. It seemed like a normal snake, coiled on the ground watching me. I moved to the right to take a wide berth around it, it swung its head to the right. My heartbeat increased. That was fine, I'd just go around the other way. I took two steps to the left. Sure enough, the snake moved to the left. Now I was worried. My heartbeat sped up a little more. I took a step back. This time, I'd go back to the waterfall and wait for Mr. Mittens. If this was a normal snake, maybe it would be gone before my cat arrived.

As I went to turn around, the snake slithered forward. Once it was uncoiled, it began to grow. Shit. I gave Mr. Mittens a mental scream, and I started to run. The snake continued to grow. An enormous head punched through the trees next to me and blocked the path. It wasn't a snake. My heart beat so fast, I felt lightheaded. I slid to a stop.

Bright yellow eyes froze me in place. The slitted pupils of the reptile thinned to almost nothing in the bright light of the noon sun and focused on me. I called for my cat again. I began to focus almost frantically on the creature's fine scales. They lay with precision, so tight against each other they appeared almost drawn on with a fine pencil. Overall, the creature was red, but up close, each scale was almost a rainbow of reds. I noticed a fine pattern along the top of the head and the neck, a slightly darker shade that formed a pattern like a diamondback rattler. I swallowed hard.

I looked carefully away and followed the sinuous neck

behind me, which had grown and flattened trees on either side of its immense body. It had four legs and a set of neatly folded wings. This wasn't a snake. It was a dragon. My knees almost gave way. What did Mr. Mittens say about dragons? Oh yeah, they were exactly what the legends said. Big scaly reptiles that breathed fire and collected hordes.

This creature was so gargantuan, even Mr. Mittens in his Splintercat form couldn't do anything against it. I was going to get eaten, and if Mr. Mittens showed up soon, I'd get him eaten, too.

Remembering that I kept reminding Mr. Mittens to talk before he killed, I addressed the dragon—even though neither I nor my cat had a chance of killing it.

"Hi. I'm Brigid. How can I help you?" I asked politely. I figured it couldn't hurt. Maybe I'd get a couple of seconds before it ate me.

A puff of smoke billowed from its nostrils. Then, like all the other magical creatures I'd met, namely my cat and Brightfeather, it spoke into my mind.

Hello Brigid, Fae lord of this land. You may call me Goch.

Okay. What? The dragon spoke. Did that mean it wasn't going to eat me?

"How do you know I'm the lord of this land?" I choked out. Before I died, I should at least get information from him.

The Splintercat said I should introduce myself. I've been granted asylum here.

I tilted my head at him.

"Why did you seek asylum?" I was curious now. Surely this wasn't a case of a bad marriage like Brightfeather's.

I have angered my wing, and I've been exiled, he stated, a hint of sadness in his mental voice.

"I'm very sorry. May I ask what you were exiled for?"

JILLEEN DOLBEARE

My mind went to a group of dragons attacking Oregon because I didn't ask the right questions.

His eyes closed slightly, and I could feel his shame.

I failed in battle. I am considered a dreamer, and I caused harm to befall another because I was dreaming when I should have been paying attention to the fight.

"Oh. I'm very sorry, Goch. You are welcome here. Is the red snake the shape you chose to show if a human comes along?"

Yes. I'm sorry I frightened you. I was trying to get your attention.

"Thank you. There aren't any red snakes in Oregon, at least that I know of, so I was concerned that you were an imported, venomous snake."

I am venomous! he said eagerly.

That wasn't really helpful, but I gave him a wan smile. "I'm sure that will come in handy."

Just then, Mr. Mittens came galloping up.

What is wrong? he asked.

Afraid to anger my new dragon responsibility, I mind-spoke back. *You failed to explain this, and I was afraid when he plopped in my path.*

Mr. Mittens's eyes flicked to Goch. *Hmpf,* he said. *I asked you to wait until I could inform the lord of the land,* he addressed the dragon.

Goch continued to look ashamed, his huge head drooped, which was difficult when it was inches from the ground. *Forgive me, my lord.*

I rolled my eyes, this "lord of the land" thing was growing old quickly. "Goch," I said aloud. "You do not have to address me as lord or lady. I'm Brigid. Please, make yourself at home, just remember, you should use your snake form if anyone that you don't know is around. You may show your true self to me, Mr. Mittens, and my friend Megan. I'll introduce you later."

Goch's head rose at that. His eyes widened. I got the distinct impression that Goch was young for his kind and still sought recognition and was eager to please. *Thank you, my...um, Brigid! I'll be the most perfect dragon!*

I gave him a small nod to acknowledge him. Goch spread his massive wings, and with a tremendous leap, launched himself into the air. The wind from the beat of his mighty wings almost knocked me down, but I recovered and watched the dragon disappear over my trees. I sighed.

"Is there enough room and food here for a dragon?" I asked my silly cat.

Mr. Mittens looked away.

"What do dragons eat?" I asked, hands on my hips.

Well. His eyes darted to the left. *They eat whatever they wish. You saw how big that one was, and he is only half grown.*

"That is not an answer."

He huffed. *They eat meat. Lots of meat. I think that I'll have to teach him to realm walk so he can hunt elsewhere.*

Great, there wasn't nearly enough food here. "If he has to be taught to realm walk, that means he's from..."

Yes, dragons live in this realm. Mr. Mittens finished my thought.

I shivered. Crap. "How, where?"

They are rare beings. Only a few hundred are left. That is why I granted Goch a home on your land. His voice was soft and sad in my mind.

My annoyance faded. That made sense, I'd have done the same. Instead of telling him off, I said, "Thanks for talking before killing."

Hmpf.

I'd have to ponder on dragons for a while. I'd always

79

thought the idea of dragons must have come from some ancient human seeing dinosaur bones or something instead of a real honest to God flying lizard. This was no pterodactyl, either. Well, as I'd learned, there are stranger things in heaven and earth, or however that Hamlet quote went. I shrugged and followed my cat down the trail towards home. At least my new life was never boring.

Chapter Eight

Even though it was lunchtime, Megan was warming her hands around a cup of coffee when Mr. Mittens and I walked into the kitchen.

"Hey! How was your first magic lesson?" she asked with a yawn.

"Did you know that there are dragons in North America?" I replied.

She sputtered. And the coffee she'd been sipping came spurting out of her mouth and over the kitchen table.

I frowned at her. "I guess that's a no."

"Dragons?" She was awake now.

I sighed. "By the way, we have a new creature courtesy of Brigid, Fae Lord." I looked pointedly at my cat.

His blue eyes gazed up at me without shame, and he jumped up on the counter and looked at the fridge. He didn't even bother to talk to me. Just did the bossy cat thing. I got out a clean dish.

"A dragon?" Megan asked hopefully. Then she frowned. "This isn't going to be disappointing like the unicorn, is it?"

"I sure hope not. But in this case, I don't know if that's a good thing or a bad one."

"Why don't you start at the beginning."

So, while I prepared Mr. Mittens's premium meal, I recounted the whole day starting with my first lesson.

"Huh." She thought for a moment, her eyes distant. "You know…"

I put up a hand, because I knew where this was going already. "We do not ride sentient creatures that can eat us."

"You shut that down way too fast," Megan said. "It's almost like you already considered it."

"Well, a telepathic dragon—of course I *went* there."

"You're sure we can't ask?"

I shook my head. "You can ask if you dare. Just remember he's a *teenage* dragon. I don't trust human teenagers to drive, let alone fly me around."

"There's that. Damn." She blew a stray hair out of her face. "This was my chance!" She flung up her hands and shook her head. "I'm never gonna fight Thread now."

I grinned, joining in. "You can still fly to the Red Star, I'm sure."

"Hell, no! I know how well that went."

"Guess you should go back to harping then." I laughed.

"You know I can't sing for shit." She mopped up the coffee from the table.

"Oh, yes, I do."

She threw the damp rag at me. We devolved into giggles, the ridiculousness of the situation getting to us.

We made lunch and ate. Mr. Mittens had finished his meal earlier and was curled up on my lap, getting stray scratches and head rubs. As we were sitting there, finishing our food, Megan said, "I've been thinking about your bed-and-breakfast idea."

I raised my eyebrows at her. "Yeah?"

"Instead of doing a straight, boring, basic B&B, why don't we cater to the supernatural community?"

I stopped chewing and swallowed. "What do you mean?" I'd kinda had this thought, too, but I hadn't fleshed it out.

"Well, just in this small town, you have a good-sized werewolf pack and a large coven of witches. Plus, there's enough weirdness going on around here that you know there are all kinds of other types, and not just from this 'realm.' Don't other races vacation? If I was a city werewolf, wouldn't I like four hundred untouched acres to run in for my two weeks holiday every year?"

"Eight hundred," I said off-hand, deep in thought.

"Eight then. Geesh."

One of the ideas I'd thought of, once Gabe was rescued and the witches were subdued, was to open up the B&B idea to include not just humanoid races, but magical creatures.

"Two hundred of those acres are an old dairy farm. It's been out of commission and is overgrown, but I'd like to change that into a kind of stable for magical creatures as well." I looked at her, and she narrowed her eyes at me.

"You already planned on doing this."

"Sort of, I haven't gotten very far, but as the vice-president of Lady Brigid, Fae Lord, Enterprises, LLC you should write up your ideas and present them at the next board meeting," I said with a fake English accent.

She raised her hand. "First item is to change the company name, the current one's much too long and overly descriptive."

"Added to the agenda." I made a mark in the air.

"Mr. Mittens, as the resident realm walker, would you in your travels, enjoy an inn set up with your needs in mind?"

He yawned, the heavy meal and pets setting him on the path to dream land. "Would there be premium cuts of fish, chicken, pork, and beef, with a side of cream available?"

"Yes." I rolled my eyes.

"It sounds lovely." He nodded back off.

Then, while the idea was fresh, we both brought out our computers and started writing up ideas and plans. I felt better about this than the new computer business idea. This fit my new life, the one I'd made for myself, free of Evan, and I was excited about it. We had one more day before we met with Gabe again, and then we'd defeat the evil witch coven, save Gabe for good, and have a plan to open a place that catered to others like me. Everything was looking up.

———

Since Megan and I were excited about the new plans, I thought that we'd better go see the old dairy and what kind of shape it was in. I'd had such a hard time getting my house renovated, I couldn't imagine what I'd have to do to get the dairy revamped into a livable space. I had a Splintercat, a griffin, and a dragon living on my property, and if I had that great a variety of clientele, I wasn't even sure how to house them. It's not like they all came in one convenient size.

We waited until Mr. Mittens was done sleeping off his lunch, and since it was a lovely day, decided to walk out to the dairy.

"Do you know the way?" I asked my cat.

He "hmpfed" at me, and I cringed. *You are the Fae lord of*

the land; you should be able to find a specific blade of grass whenever you wish, he chastised.

"OK, I'll give it a go," I said. I'd die of embarrassment if I got us lost—again.

Megan saw the uncertainty on my face because she smiled. "No biggy, it'll be an adventure!"

"Great!" I said with false cheer.

It was warm enough for short sleeves. So, we walked out the door and into my woods, wearing jeans, t-shirts, and boots for the inevitable mud or muck we'd encounter on the way. Even though I led the way, Mr. Mittens strolled along for protection. You never knew what you'd find in my woods.

The dairy was on the western side of the property. I don't think it had been an active dairy since the seventies, so it didn't have much modern equipment. However, there were a lot of buildings. I didn't know much about dairies, but I had grown up in a dairy town, so I had a general idea what each structure was for. To one side was a modest farmhouse, which had been used as a rental in years past. Then, there was the milking barn, that was obvious, the feeding barn for winter when the cows weren't at pasture, the calving barn, and a covered hay barn. There were various sheds for tools and equipment, and fenced pastures. Everything was grown over and returning to nature. At least the large structures looked solid.

"Boy," Megan said. "This looks like a lot of work."

I nodded. I was a little discouraged because it did look like a lot of work. There was the cleaning and taming of the pastures and the outside of each building. I could probably handle the grounds with my magic, but I needed someone to come in and check out the structures and make sure they were as sound as they looked, and then an idea on how to turn them into creature stables. I didn't really have a clue for that one.

"Mr. Mittens, do you have any idea what mythical creatures would need in a structure?"

He turned his periwinkle gaze at me. *Shelter from the elements, a soft bed, and plenty of food.*

That sounded about right. He wasn't picky where he slept, since he slept on the table, on the floor, in the middle of my bed, really any place he felt tired. For a supernatural being, he sure acted like a regular cat.

"That's helpful." I rolled my eyes, making sure only Megan could see.

I took a few pics with my phone camera, and we went to look inside each building. We started with the barns, since the house would be good for a caretaker or two but wouldn't be part of the guest facilities. We took more pics and talked about what would need to be done. After we checked out the outbuildings and barns, we headed to the house.

The door still had the realtor's lock on it. I had the code; I just hadn't been here to check it out since I'd moved. It wasn't high on my list. I punched in the code on the lockbox and took out the key. The door squeaked eerily when I opened it, and we were greeted with dust and cobwebs. The power wasn't on, but enough light filtered through the uncovered windows, that it wasn't much of an issue.

The house also looked solid, and I was grateful. It would need a whole new electric and maybe a plumbing update, but other than new appliances, paint, and flooring, and of course a thorough cleaning, it looked great. I needed to get an inspector in to check if it was safe to have the water and plumbing turned back on, but since the house had been lived in within the last five years, unlike the dairy, it was probably not an issue.

It was a simple two-story farmhouse, three bedrooms upstairs, the living room, a half bath, kitchen and mudroom on the main floor, and a full basement. I doubted the basement would be light enough to explore without the electricity being on, but Megan and I had the flashlights on our phones, so we decided to brave the spiders and check it out. When I suggested it to Mr. Mittens, he gave an annoyed swish of his tail, but his curiosity won out, and he followed us down the basement stairs.

Like a lot of basements on the coast, it smelled dank and musty. I wondered why there was a full basement, since the water table was so high. It was a rare thing to find here. But it was extra space to be used, so down we went. It was dark, and our phone flashlights barely pushed back the gloom. It was spooky too, and I shivered. The short sleeve t-shirt I was wearing was not enough after the warmth of the bright sunlit day and the upper floors.

"It's cold down here," Megan echoed my thoughts.

I nodded. Just then, Mr. Mittens froze. I froze too. Anything that scared my cat, doubly scared me.

"Megan, get behind me," I said.

She turned and frowned at me, but then she noticed my cat and slid behind me and out of his way.

"What's down here?" I asked him.

I'm not sure, but it feels bad, he answered.

"Bad, how?"

But he didn't answer. There was a low growl emanating from his direction, which sent more icy shivers trailing down my back. I motioned for Megan to start back up the stairs. She scooted one foot back, and I followed, keeping my eyes peeled for whatever my cat was sensing.

Nothing but darkness.

Run! Mr. Mittens announced into our minds.

Megan turned to start up the stairs but tripped and fell onto them. Since I was right behind her, I fell on her. Which was a good thing, because as I fell, something dark passed over my head, brushing my hair. I yipped.

Mr. Mittens followed, still in Ragdoll form, but his eyes flashed, and his claws were out, and they were much larger than those of a regular house cat. I rolled off Megan, and she started to scramble up the stairs. I got my feet back under me, but I turned to see what Mr. Mittens was chasing. I saw a shadowy figure, but with the lack of light, I couldn't tell what it was. Now I was good and aware that there was something down here with us, I realized that the atmosphere had become heavy, and fear was pressing me down. Megan was at the top of the stairs.

"Come on, Bridge!"

I shook my head. I wasn't going to let something I couldn't see dictate what I did. I had light magic. Time to illuminate the issue. I hadn't practiced with it much, so when I called it up, it filled the basement full of light so bright, it temporarily blinded me. Mr. Mittens squawked, I'm sure it really hurt his cat eyes.

After my eyes adjusted, I saw what he'd been chasing, and I wished I hadn't. I didn't know what it was, but it had a shiny black spider body like a black widow, but a human-like face. Only the human face had spider mandibles, fangs, and four jeweled eyes. The light had also stunned it, luckily, because I didn't want to get Mr. Mittens eaten. It was frozen, but I could see the tiny hairs along its legs quiver, and I knew it would be moving again soon. I wondered once more why my cat hadn't transformed into his larger Splintercat form.

"What's wrong, Mr. Mittens?" I called out.

He shook his head like you did if you're disoriented. *The creature bit me*, he slurred into my mind.

"Uh oh."

It appears to have injected me with some kind of neurotoxin. I can't transform.

He wobbled. I wondered if it would kill him.

"Let's get you out of here," I said. "Before that thing comes after us again."

It's afraid of the light, he added, then fell over on his side.

A wave of fear ran through me. I didn't want anything bad to happen to my cat. What would I do without him?

The spider moved a leg. I blasted another wave of light magic, and the spider froze again, the hairs on its legs vibrating. I scooped up Mr. Mittens and held him like a baby. He was limp. Too limp. This wasn't the typical Ragdoll flop, this was boneless. I pressed my hand against his stomach, it rose and fell slightly, weakly. I raced up the stairs and slammed the door at the top.

"Megan, he's been bitten," I yelled as I raced forward through the kitchen and out the side door. "Let's go!"

She gasped but fell in behind me.

"Call the vet, see what we should do for a black widow bite," I called as we ran back towards the house.

"On it." She was punching things into her phone, then I saw her select and dial. She told the technician the issue and waited to be connected to the vet.

She was quiet, listening. Then she said, "OK," and hung up.

"He said, wash it with soap, put ice on the bite, and get him there ASAP, they are waiting with antivenin."

"Shit, I don't know if that thing had black widow venom, it wasn't natural!"

"I know. Hopefully, they have general medicine."

We were both huffing and puffing. Frankly, I walked around a lot, but I only ran if I was chased. Megan did some mild jogging sometimes, so she was better off than I was, but I didn't want my cat to die. I dug in and kept on.

Mr. Mittens was moaning now—both in my mind and out loud. He was panting as well. Not good signs. We surged into the house. I washed the wound on his leg, and Megan grabbed ice. I snatched my purse and the keys, and we piled into my car and raced down the long drive to the main road and help.

Chapter Nine

By the time we pulled into the vet, Mr. Mittens's leg was swollen, he was salivating badly, and he was having muscle tremors. I rubbed his head, trying to give him comfort, but he was out of it.

A vet tech took him from me, shaved his other leg, and inserted an IV. The vet came in.

"Tell me what bit him," he asked, looking at me over his glasses.

"I'm not sure. I thought I saw a spider scurry away," I replied vaguely. I wanted to tell him, but he wouldn't believe me.

"The bite is large, but I only see one puncture hole, so hopefully, he didn't get a full venom load. It helps that he has a large body. Without knowing the spider, I don't know which antivenom to give."

I bit back a sob. "What can we do?"

"We treat the symptoms and hope he's strong."

I hugged myself and looked at Mr. Mittens. He was strong, right?

The vet put him on fluids and pain meds. Apparently, spider venom could create a lot of pain. That explained the groaning. I sat next to him and stroked his head. He was too strong for this, no way could a stupid spider bring him down. He fought unicorns and commanded dragons. I was gonna squash that spider thing—although it was probably over thirty pounds. I'd get a big ass boot. If I had too, I'd burn the house to the ground. I could bring in a manufactured home for the caretakers. No one wanted an infestation of spiders or venomous spider things.

We waited with him for hours. I'd cried until my eyes were almost swollen shut, and Megan wasn't much better. The vet and the tech constantly checked on him. They were about to move him into the back and kick us out when Mr. Mittens's eyes fluttered open.

I need to transform. A weak Mr. Mittens said into my mind. I bolted upright. I looked at the vet. He continued to frown at whatever he was looking at.

"Will it help?"

The vet gave me a strange look, and I cringed. I'd said that out loud.

Yes. My size will change, and the poison will disburse quicker.

"*I'll get the vet out of here, unless you want to go home?*" I replied to him in my mind, concentrating so my mind magic would work.

Yes. Home. His voice went quiet, and I saw he was asleep again.

"What are his chances if I take him home?" I asked the vet. My voice quavering.

"I can't promise anything. He'll be in pain once the meds wear off, and he'll need fluids. If you feel you can do that at home, he can go. But I don't recommend it."

The vet didn't understand I had a magical cat. But I

had to do what I could to save my protector and friend. I nodded. "I'm gonna take him home. If anything changes, I'll bring him back. I just think he'll be happier there."

The vet's expression said he disapproved, but he didn't argue. He just nodded and had the vet tech prepare a take home kit with medication and a bag of Lactated Ringer's for subcutaneous fluids, which they showed me how to administer. I took the bag of stuff and handed it to Megan. I picked up and cradled Mr. Mitten's limp body gently in my arms, and we walked back to the car.

I shouldn't have taken him to the vet at all, but I was so scared. Megan was, too. He laid in my lap, limp as a wet rag. His breathing was rough and shallow, and his drool wet my leg. I was still scared, but I believed that transforming was better for him. He was magical. He had to get better.

When we got to the house, I took him in and laid him on my king-sized bed. He'd need the large space. He sighed when I laid him down but didn't awaken.

"Mr. Mittens, wake up," I said softly.

He moaned.

"Wake up," I said louder. Worried now that he hadn't stirred.

I looked at Megan; she frowned.

I was starting to panic.

I put a knee on the bed and shook him gently.

What? A grouchy voice croaked into my mind.

"We're home. You can transform," I answered.

He stretched out to his full length, and his body shimmered and went right back to his Ragdoll form.

"Mr. Mittens? Can you transform?" I asked nervously.

In answer, he rolled over and lay panting. Then, he pulled his feet up and stood, wobbling on the bed. He weaved back and forth as he tried to maintain his balance. His head hung low, and his eyes looked dull.

He shook his head. Panic gripped my heart. What if he couldn't do it? Would he die? I reached out a hand to steady him.

He huffed and shimmered again. This time when he failed, he collapsed back on his side, exhausted.

I need a minute, he said. *I'm weak.*

"What can I do for you?" I asked, willing to try anything so he could get better.

He was silent, and I panicked. I leaned in and put my hand on his side to see if he was still breathing. I wished with all my might he could transform and get well. Under my hand, his body grew. I stepped back, as the shimmer over his body exploded, and his Splintercat form lay panting on my bed, filling the entire thing.

Thank you, Brigid, he said. *I needed the boost.*

"I helped you?" I asked, surprised.

Yes. You lent me some of your magic. It was what I needed. Now I must rest. His panting had slowed, and his drooping eyes slammed shut.

I looked at Megan. She shrugged.

"I guess we're out of a bed tonight," she said with a wry smile on her face.

"Yeah, I guess so." I'd sleep in the car if it meant Mr. Mittens would get better, so I didn't care. We laughed—the stress leaving our bodies. I was shaking. I turned off the bedroom light and closed the door—not tight, in case he needed to get out in the night, but enough so the light and the noise from our talking wouldn't disturb him. His breathing had deepened, and he snored. I grinned, relieved, and followed Megan into the kitchen.

"Maybe your bed will be here tomorrow," I began.

She nodded. "Yeah, but we're out of luck today."

"No, we're in luck if Mr. Mittens is OK."

"You're right. I'm starving. Let's eat."

I nodded. As we ate, the exhaustion hit. It was late, and I had to get up and face my magic teacher, meet with Gabe, and come up with a plan to defeat the witches. I needed to rest. I didn't even have a couch to lay down on, and I doubted I could sleep on the hard floor and wake up refreshed.

"If you can stay with Mr. Mittens, I'm going to run to town and get us a couple of air mattresses," I said after we were done.

"Are you sure? I can go if you're too tired," Megan offered.

I shook my head. Even though I was exhausted, my mind buzzed, and I hoped the car ride would relax me. I'd take her with me, but I really didn't want Mr. Mittens to be left alone. I checked on him. He'd turned over. He was lying on his back, his front legs straight up, but relaxed paws flopped down, and his rear legs stretched out like a person. He was drooling on my pillow. His breathing was smoother, and his snoring had died down to deep breathing. I breathed a sigh of relief, grabbed my purse, and headed to the store.

Chapter Ten

I picked out two of the best queen air mattresses sold at Freddie's and a box of pastries for my magic teacher and checked out. I took my packages to the car and loaded them up. I had coffee for the morning, so hopefully, this would be enough to keep me on Dana's good side.

It started to rain, hard, on the way home. That wasn't surprising, I lived in the temperate rainforest on the north central Oregon coast. I turned onto 101 and started south towards my house. As I passed through the green light crossing Highway 6, I saw a truck coming down it. I accelerated because it looked like he wasn't going to stop. He wasn't. He sped up. My heart hammered, and I screamed as I punched the accelerator. I couldn't get out of the way or maneuver in time. I had all of this magic, things were finally going my way, and I was about to die in a car accident. The truck bashed into the side of my car. My car bucked up and slid and spun across the road. I was yanked back and forth against my seat belt, and all the curtain airbags deployed.

I sat there, blinking. Trying to figure out what

happened. Several cars stopped, and someone pounded on my window. I hit the button and rolled the window down. I must have still been stunned, because it took me a minute to decide what the woman was saying to me. Then, like a fog lifting, I heard her. "Are you OK?"

Was I? I blinked some more. I couldn't quite decide or get the words together. I was alive, that was good. I grabbed the door handle and opened the door. The woman came around it. She looked me over.

"I'm a nurse. I saw the wreck."

"OK," I said, finally finding my voice.

I unlatched the seat belt and swung my legs out. When I tried to stand, they wanted to buckle, but I tamed them and stood. I was sore, but nothing seemed broken, and I wasn't bleeding. My car was a mess though. The side was bashed in, and the wheels were canted from being pushed so hard across the street and into a curb. I frowned at it. I was swaying, I think, because someone grabbed my arm and maneuvered me, so I was sitting in the driver's seat again.

"Thanks." I looked around. "What happened?" I asked next.

The lady helping me frowned. "That truck was going fast. Way too fast. It sped off after hitting you. The guy over there…" She pointed. "Called the cops."

Once she said that, I noticed the sirens, and the crowds of looky-loos watching me from the sidewalk, a few with phones taking pics. I blushed, suddenly embarrassed by all the attention.

"Umm, I've got to go," I said to the lady, and moved to swing my legs in and start up the car.

"Honey, you aren't going anywhere. That car is done for, and you are not thinking straight."

I remembered the car and nodded. I put my hand up to

my head and felt a huge lump on the side of my forehead. When the truck hit me, I must have smacked it on the side window. Or the curtain airbag had hit me. I didn't know. "Ok," I said.

The police and ambulance arrived. The police took witness statements and asked me what happened. I told them the best I could remember. Then the ambulance put me on their stretcher, loaded me up, and checked me out before transporting me to the small hospital in town. I had one of them call Megan.

Once there, they did all the doctor things, including a CT of my head to check for a concussion. It was clear. I was surprised, because I knew I was still goofy and acting erratically. I hated that Megan had to leave Mr. Mittens to come and get me, and I had her wait an hour before she came so I would be cleared and ready to leave. Luckily it was a slow night at the ER, and I was treated quickly. By the time Megan arrived to pick me up, I'd been released and some of the events came flooding back to me.

Megan was quiet until we got in her car. Apparently, mine was totaled.

"What happened?" she asked softly after I told her my head was pounding.

I looked at her for a moment and then back to the road. I was shivering, the aftereffects hitting me hard. "I was just going through the light."

I looked at the oncoming headlights and shrunk back against the door. She reached out and gripped my hand.

"It was a big crew cab F-350. I saw it at the last moment. When I realized, it wasn't going to stop for the light, I punched the accelerator. I think it was planning to hit my door." I looked at her. "Whoever there were was trying to kill me."

Megan's knuckles turned white on the wheel. "That son of a whore."

I chuckled. "Yeah."

"Did you see the driver at all?"

I thought back. Yes, I did. At the last moment, once I knew I wasn't going to avoid a collision, I saw his face clearly. It was the kicker from the night the witches stole my ice magic.

"That sadistic bastard!" I said loud enough that Megan jumped.

"Who?"

"The guy that hit me is the same cruel bastard that beat me up before you got here. A freaking witch!"

She huffed, angrily. "What's their problem?"

"Sofia," I answered simply. "I'm probably on the coven's hit list."

"Don't they need you alive to steal your magic?" she asked.

I shrugged. I didn't know. Something to ask Dana tomorrow. I slumped. Dana. How was I going to do a magic lesson with the Fae teacher from hell?

I must have groaned.

"What's wrong?" Megan asked anxiously, expecting me to collapse from my injuries on the ride home. I was sore and battered, but not really injured, not like the witches had done to me before.

"I have a magic lesson tomorrow, and I don't know if I can do it."

"Oh."

"Yeah."

"Well, I got all your stuff out of the car before I came over, so at least you can sleep comfortably!"

That jolted me. "How's Mr. Mittens?" I asked belatedly.

"He was still snoring when I left."

"Good." I breathed out in relief. "I don't think I'm thinking straight."

Megan barked out a laugh. "Really?"

"You aren't very funny," I grumped. I pressed my fingers to the side of my head, feeling the nice sized lump. "My brains got a good sloshing."

She sobered. "I know. That must have been so scary."

"I don't think I was. Scared I mean. It happened too fast. I only had time to accelerate, and that saved my life. The truck hit the side behind me, instead of into me."

"Yeah, the car was smushed behind your door. I had to get everything out of the back from the passenger side," she agreed.

"I liked that car. I'm adding it to the list of items that I'm taking out of Sofia's hide."

"You do that. She's seriously making her way onto my list, too." Megan sniffed.

She reached out a hand and squeezed mine when I slipped it into hers. I smiled at her. She turned onto the long gravel drive up to the house, and after she parked, I hurried in to check on Mr. Mittens.

He was still asleep, but he'd rolled over, so his legs weren't in the air. He was on his side, his breath sounded normal now, and I breathed a sigh of relief. He'd make it. I brushed a cautious swipe down his spotted fur, and he twitched slightly, but didn't awaken.

I walked out and partially shut the door so he could have as much quiet as possible.

"I'm going to call Luke," Megan said.

"Because of the wreck?" I was baiting her a little. She probably just wanted to talk to him.

"Yeah, if the witches are going after you, that means

Sofia is up to something, and they might know what," she replied.

That actually made sense. I really wasn't thinking clearly. She called and let Luke know, and he said that the wolves would check it out.

Megan and I made up our beds in the huge entryway, and exhausted, I fell asleep.

Chapter Eleven

I awoke and rolled off the air mattress onto my hands and knees. I struggled to my feet, every muscle in my body screaming. The wreck must have jostled me around more than I thought. I stretched slowly. It took the walk to the bathroom and into the kitchen before I could walk without shuffling.

I brushed my hair and teeth, got a cup of coffee and a pastry. In the middle of my breakfast, a flash of light announced the entrance of Dana.

"Are you ready?" she asked imperiously.

I sighed and waved at the pastries. Her eyes lit up at the treats, and she selected one with a sigh of pleasure. I grinned, facing away from her so she wouldn't see. She wolfed it down along with two more.

"This realm has delightful food," she remarked.

"We do have good pastries," I said.

She gave herself time to enjoy one more before barking at me to move out.

When I groaned involuntarily as I stood, she frowned at

me. "What is wrong?" She spoke sharply.

"Witches keep trying to kill me," I answered truthfully.

Her face reflected rage, her green skin blushing darkly, her eyes narrowing. "Who is this witch?" Her voice was deeper and more resonant.

"The same one that kicked my ass a week ago. A member of the coven that is trying to steal my magic."

She grew quiet, thoughtful. "Then we shall, what did you say? Kick their asses first."

That's what I was talking about.

Megan looked at me, her eyes wide. She mouthed over the Kelpie's head, "What the hell?"

I shrugged. "OK," I said.

I checked on Mr. Mittens before we left for the waterfall. He stretched and hopped off the bed from his huge Splintercat form into his Ragdoll.

I'm hungry, he muttered.

"Megan is making your breakfast right now. I have a date with my magic teacher. We'll be at the waterfall."

When you return, I request your assistance in destroying the creature that bit me.

I nodded, wondering what I could do, but I owed that spider thing a good smoosh with my boot.

As we walked to the waterfall, Dana asked me what happened. I gave her a blow by blow. Of course, that required that I explain what a car and truck were which was interesting. I agreed to take her for a ride after our lesson.

Today wasn't as beautiful as the day before. The sky was overcast and threatened to rain.

Dana had been deep in thought during the second half of the walk after my tale. Just before we took the turn off the trail to the waterfall, we stopped at the spring for a drink. A red snake lay next to it, his eyes alert, looking at me for permission to speak.

"Hello, Goch, how are you today?" I asked politely with a side glance at Dana to gauge her reaction to the bright red serpent.

She held her hands aloft, as though she were going to smite the creature.

"Stop!" I yelled at her, and she glared at me.

"That creature is masking his true form."

"I know. He's a dragon. I've asked him to use his snake form around strangers."

"Hmmm."

"Goch, you may show your true form to Dana. She is a Kelpie from the Fae realm."

"Half," Dana added.

I nodded. I didn't think that Goch cared, I just wanted him to know she wasn't human.

He unfurled to his full length and grew into his immense dragon form. "Thank you, Lady Brigid," he said in his eager to please voice.

"It's just Brigid. How may I help you, Goch?" I asked, staring up and up into his face.

"Brightfeather told me about the witches and asked me to report to you if I saw any strange humans come onto your land."

"What did you see?" I asked, becoming concerned. Were those damned witches still sneaking onto my land?

"Two were looking around the house earlier this morning."

"Oh?" I sure hoped he didn't eat anyone. Unless it was Sofia. But it could be someone like a meter reader or something, and I wasn't sure how to explain that to the power company.

"Were they in a car or truck?" I asked.

He looked at me for a minute. "I don't know what that is."

Right, magical creature. Why would he know the terms car and truck?

"Thanks, Goch. You did the right thing by letting me know."

His eyes lit up. He was so eager to please, and he ate up the praise. "I'll keep an eye out!"

I smiled up at him. He leapt up and flew off, the dust and forest detritus swirling up around us.

"You have a dragon?" Dana asked, flatly.

"I don't own him, but he's welcome on my land. He's just a kid," I added, quickly.

"Dragons are very useful creatures," she said, the light of avarice burning in her eyes.

"What do you mean?" I was growing concerned with the way she watched Goch fly off, and I was worried she would try something that would harm the young dragon. I vowed to keep her and the dragon separate when she was here.

"No matter." She brushed it away. "Let's go to your seat of power."

It may not matter to her, but now I had to think of ways to keep Goch away from her. I didn't want him to be injured or killed because of me. He'd come to me for help.

We finished the journey to the waterfall, and I prepared myself for another mentally draining day making tiny gains.

"Do you have access to shadow magic?" she asked.

"I do, but I don't know how to use it."

"If the witches are making attempts on your life, it would be best to skip elemental control and move into shielding first and then offensive magic."

Yes! I thought that would be amazing, but I just nodded at Dana.

"Shadow is the perfect shield," she added.

I looked away for a moment and when I looked back, Dana was gone. "Dana?" I asked, confused.

"Yes?" Her voice hadn't moved from where she was, but she was not visible.

Her form popped back into my vision.

"Was that shadow magic?" I asked, amazed.

"Yes."

"How does it work?"

"Shadows are naturally concealing. So, the magic just enhances that quality. Let your shadow magic envelope you in its warm embrace, and you'll fade from view."

We practiced for our allotted time, and finally, I was able to call up and wrap myself in shadow so completely that Dana pronounced me, "adequate." I expected Dana to disappear in a flash, but instead she stood and stared at me. Right, she wanted to ride in a "metal beast of burden." I nodded in silent agreement and headed back home to face that and all the other tasks of the day.

I opened my back door and called for Mr. Mittens. Megan's car was gone, so I assumed she'd gone to town on an errand. Since my vehicle was wrecked, I couldn't take Dana until Megan returned. I made some lunch for the three of us, Dana, myself, and my cat, and before we finished eating, a delivery van arrived. Mattresses. Dana agreed to stay in the kitchen out of view, while the delivery guys hauled several mattresses up the stairs and laid them on the awaiting beds. One step closer to opening my magical B&B. Megan's mattress was a couple of orders of magnitude nicer than the guest ones, and the delivery guys placed it on the bed frame in her newly cleaned and organized room.

I looked around. We were so close. A few more items to cross off in the guest rooms, but I had a list of handymen to call for those, and the house was done. Now to get a crew for the creature quarters, but before that could be done, we had to rid ourselves of a nasty venomous beastie.

Megan came back soon after the mattress guys left, and I showed her my new trick.

"That's the coolest!" she exclaimed. "You can turn invisible!"

"Not really, I'm just cloaked."

"Like the Predator?"

I frowned. "You watched those movies?" I asked. "I thought you only watched rom-coms and action flicks."

"I watch sci-fi and fantasy movies too."

"Uh, the last time I asked you to go with me, you said, and I quote, 'It's too scary. I'll have nightmares.'"

"I got over it."

"Uh huh."

"OK, you caught me. When I told you that, I had a blind date, and I didn't want to tell you in case it was a total disaster."

"Was it?"

"Yes, that's why you don't know about it," she huffed.

"That's ridiculous. As your best friend, you can't deny me the right to mock and denigrate a terrible blind date."

"In my defense, you were distracted by your divorce, I was sparing you from the disaster of my own love life."

"What about Luke?" I asked suddenly.

She blushed. "He asked me out for Friday, if everything goes well tonight with the Gabe thing and there's nothing else going on."

I smiled at her; a thrill of excitement ran through me for my friends. They'd be so cute together. "I'm excited for you, Luke is great."

"Thanks. It'll be weird knowing I'm dating a guy who transforms into a giant wolf, but it's also sort of exciting, like the ultimate bad boy."

"I get that." I nodded at her. It was true, you got the bad boy who treated you well. The perfect man. Couldn't beat that. Then, because Dana was watching our interaction and glaring at me, I asked, "Can I borrow your car?"

"Sure, why?"

"I promised Dana a ride. She's never been in a car."

"I thought Fae couldn't be near 'cold iron'?"

I looked at Dana. "Are you alright being inside an iron beast?" I rolled my eyes inwardly that I had to say that.

"I'm only half Fae," she said stiffly.

That didn't answer my question, but I didn't dare ask her anything else.

"OK, let's go." Megan tossed me her keys, and I led Dana out to the car.

I walked to the driver's side, and Dana followed me. Ugh. I walked her around to the passenger side and showed her how to open the door, where to sit, and how to buckle the seat belt. Then I went back to the driver's side and climbed in.

"I'm gonna push this button," I said demonstrating, but not pushing. "Once I do, the engine will start, and you'll hear it and feel it through the seat. Are you ready?"

She nodded. Her hands gripped the side of the seat, and she looked frightened—an expression I doubt her face had ever made. I pushed the button, and the engine roared to life.

Dana stiffened and jerked in surprise.

I laughed to myself and started rolling slowly around the house to the long gravel drive. I went very slow, maybe fifteen miles an hour. I couldn't really go too fast on the drive. Once I hit to the road, I turned left and sped up to fifty. Dana pressed herself into the seat as far as she could and started screaming, "Stop!"

I pulled over. "Are you alright?" I asked, my heart pounding.

"That was so fast. How is this possible?" She looked shaken. Her hands quaked, and her lips trembled with fear.

"It's not magic. It's technology."

"I don't know that word, tech-no-logy," she repeated slowly.

"It means we are good at building machines."

She nodded. Then in a flash, she disappeared. I guessed she was done with the driving lesson. I shrugged, flipped a u-ey, and returned to the house.

Once I got back, I opened the back door.

Megan looked up at me. "Where's Dana?"

I shrugged. "She didn't handle the car very well, she left."

Megan went to the back door and pulled on her high rubber boots.

"Well, you ready to go squash a nasty spider?"

I pointed to my hiking boot encased feet. "Sure am."

"What's the plan?" Megan asked.

"We go in, find it, squish it, and burn the place to the ground."

"How about we just set it on fire from outside the house?"

"I like how you think." I shuddered. I really didn't want to see that thing again, and none of us could afford a bite. It had almost taken out my Splintercat, and I didn't think anything could do that.

I don't think you can burn it, my cat added.

"Why not?" I asked.

"I think it's a Xkrgny."

"A what?"

He huffed. *A soul spider.*

"That means nothing to me." I looked at Megan.

"Me either."

We looked at him expectantly.

Hmpf. He sat and laid his tail gracefully around his feet, the shaved spot on his leg a stark contrast against his usual fluffy perfection. *A creature that can vary its presence between here and elsewhere.*

That was as clear as mud.

"Um, I still don't understand," I said.

It can slip in between realms with a thought. It's difficult to kill because it can phase from material to immaterial.

"Good hell." I put my hands on my hips and paced. "How do we kill it then?"

We must catch it when it is solidly here, he said, like it was an easy thing to do.

So armed with our cowardice, we headed out. Mr. Mittens in the lead, his floofy tail blowing in the gentle breeze.

Chapter Twelve

Instead of the cute farmhouse I'd seen the first time, the house had a sinister air. I shivered. This was all in my head. That spider thing, whatever Mr. Mittens had called it, was still there, haunting the place—apparently in more ways than one. I guess it sort of was a ghost since it could go immaterial at a whim.

We stopped and stared at the house before we marched up the few steps to the front door and pushed inside. I removed the realtor box. We'd left in such a hurry before, that it wasn't locked. I put my hand on the knob of the basement door. "Are you ready?" I asked my two companions.

I got a nod from Megan and a "*yes*" from Mr. Mittens. I twisted the knob, and the door swung open with a creak. That didn't add to the atmosphere at all. I shivered again.

I stared into the darkness of the basement. We were better prepared today, we wore headlamps, and I immediately added my light magic to act like the missing light bulbs. The basement was quiet. Where was the ugly spider?

I stepped down the wooden stairs, the creaky door was backed up with creepy creaky stairs as well. If we got rid of the spider creature, this would make a great haunted house. My heart was pounding in my ears. Megan put her hand on my shoulder, and I jumped.

"Sorry," she whispered.

"It's OK," I replied. But my skin crawled, and I resisted the urge to run my fingers through my hair and scratch all over. Images of invisible spiders and creepy crawlies flashed through my mind. My "ick" factor was on high alert.

Mr. Mittens brought up the rear, even he was being cautious after almost dying. I heard skittering, and my head whipped towards the sound in the darkest corner of the basement behind the stairs. I sped up. If it snuck up between the stairs, we wouldn't see it until it was too late.

We made it to the concrete floor and spread out, our headlamps piercing the gloom as we searched every dark corner. I whirled when I caught an old box moving out of the corner of my eye. "There!" I pointed.

The box stilled. We all faced it. "Maybe you should transform," I whispered to Mr. Mittens.

The space is too small, I can't maneuver as well in my natural form, he replied.

It would be tight, but I was freaked out about him almost dying. "Are you sure?"

Hmpf.

Where was the damn spider? I swept my head back and forth, trying to illuminate the space with my headlamp. Nothing. Had it phased? A cold feeling of being watched prickled the back of my neck, and I whirled. That creepy creature had phased behind us. Everyone else either reacted because I did or felt they were being watched as well, because they also turned, and the spider was there looking at us. It was easily the same size as Mr. Mittens in his Ragdoll form although with longer spider legs. To make it worse, it had ten legs rather than eight. Because more legs made it less creepy, right? Wrong.

It hissed at us and spat something that was yellowish green. The glob shot forward about three feet, falling short of us and hissing as it struck the concrete. Great, it was venomous and spit acid. What other nasty tricks did it have? I had a strange thought and sent out a mental call. Maybe we already had help available.

How were we going to fight this thing? We had no weapons, no ability to stop it from phasing, and it could poison us or melt us with acid. I looked at Megan. She'd always had overdeveloped arachnophobia, and she appeared frozen. I reached out a hand and squeezed hers in comfort.

The spider thing faded from view. "Maybe we should stand back-to-back," I suggested, and Mr. Mittens and Megan hurried forward, and we stood in a triangle form so we could observe the room.

"There!" Megan yelled, and sure enough the spider materialized in front of her. It stalked forward until it was in range with its acid spit, and Megan jumped out of the way just in time. It faded again.

"This was a bad idea," I said to my companions.

"Yeah," Megan agreed. Her shoulder brushed mine, and I could feel her tremble.

If we can anticipate where it will show, we'll get it, Mr. Mittens said.

"Uh…How?" I asked, but we didn't have time to worry because it appeared again. Once again, we jumped out of the way just in time. I swear the creature was playing with us, probably laughing or whatever spiders did when they found something funny.

It kept fading and reappearing, but it made a mistake. It was forming a pattern. Once it faded out again, I said, "Next time it appears, I'm going to try to hit it with my fire magic."

I got a quiet assent. We were starting to get tired.

The spider appeared, and I sent a ball of flame at it. Its four eyes widened slightly, but it faded quickly.

"Damn!" I've got to anticipate it!

I'll attempt to jump on its back, if I'm holding it down, maybe you'll get enough time to set it on fire, Mr. Mittens offered.

"I don't want to set you on fire," I responded.

I will heal faster from that than from its venom.

I cringed but nodded. "It's going to appear in front of Megan in three, two…" Mr. Mittens maneuvered to where he could easily pounce, and the spider creature began to fade in. The second before it was perfectly solid, Mr. Mittens launched his large house cat body and came down directly on the back of the shiny black carapace. The spider body sunk to the ground, its legs splayed, and I hit it with the hottest fire I could conjure. The spider screamed an eerie squealing rasp like metal being twisted and torn. Mr. Mittens leaped away and rolled the flames from his fur. I applied more fire.

The screaming stopped, and the creature melted into the concrete—black sludge and green goo being consumed by the white-hot flame.

"Awesome!" Megan exclaimed.

I shuddered but turned to her to take the fist bump.

"Mr. Mittens, is the house clean? Are there any other nasty creatures here?" The bottom line was I didn't really want to burn the house to the foundation, but I would if there was another nasty beastie here.

His eyes went still, and his inner eyelids partially closed. His little grey nose wiggled a little as he sniffed.

I don't believe so, he answered after a few minutes. *However, all I can smell is fried Xkrgny.*

"I'll take it. A fried one is better than a live one."

On that, we all agreed. We did a thorough search of the basement, overturning boxes and looking behind shelves. We found a few regular spiders and insects, but no more soul spiders. We took another turn through the house, searching for more nasties, but it appeared clean. I breathed a sigh of relief, and we went back to the house for the next task—meeting with Gabe.

On the walk back, a dragon landed in the pasture by the dairy.

"Goch!" I said, in surprise, then remembered I'd sent for him. "We handled it, sorry I called you for nothing."

My lady, there are a couple of humans at your house. Come quickly! he said, proud that he could warn me.

I thanked him, and he flew off, promising to be near, but out of sight. The three of us ran back to the house.

Chapter Thirteen

We arrived panting. There was a van parked in the gravel area behind the house next to Megan's red SUV. Two men stood on the back porch. I paused and Megan stopped with me. Mr. Mittens stood behind a tree, keeping an eye on the intruders and growling softly.

Before we stepped out of the woods and into view, I examined them. One of the men, who was short, but stockily built, scanned the yard. He had dark hair and a darker complexion, probably Hispanic. The other had his back to us. He was taller, well-built, muscular, and had white-blond hair. I froze. Scott. It had to be.

"I think the blond is Scott," I said to Megan. "I wonder what he's doing here."

"Scott, the asshole?" Megan asked.

"Yeah."

I suggest that you go back to the farm. I'll deal with the intruders, Mr. Mitten snarled.

I couldn't let that happen. Scott was a bastard, but he

wasn't anywhere near Sofia's level of evil and didn't deserve a full on Splintercat confrontation. He had no protection. He was a witch, but not one strong enough to wield magic.

"It's OK," I said to my cat. "I'll go see what he wants. You guys stay here in case something is hinky."

Megan nodded. It took a little more soothing before Mr. Mittens agreed. I stepped out of the trees and walked towards the house.

Once the other guy saw me, he elbowed Scott who turned and waved at me. I frowned. We weren't that friendly anymore, but he had kept his word after he promised me. I wondered what he wanted.

Once I was close enough, he took a step towards me and said, "Hi, Brigid."

"Hi," I said warily back. "Who's your buddy?"

Scott looked at his companion as though he'd forgotten about him. "Oh, this is Jorge, he works for me."

Jorge nodded and held out his hand. I looked at it, but then I grasped his hand and shook it cautiously.

"What do you want, Scott?" I didn't make any effort to keep the disdain out of my voice.

"Umm, well..." He thought for a moment. "I'm sorry my crew and I weren't back after the thing with my cousin, but it wasn't my fault. She forbade me to come back. I just wanted to apologize and see if you still wanted us to finish up. This is *my* business, and I don't have anything to do with her anymore."

I shook my head. I didn't trust him as far as I could throw him. "I don't think so. Send your final bill, and I think we don't ever have to see one another again," I said firmly.

Scott looked down, and I think he truly looked contrite.

"I really am sorry. I let her blind me. I was stupid. I hope you can forgive me someday. I brought Jorge because I thought you might say that. He's a good dude. He doesn't know anything about...um...Sofia or her...dealings. So, if you don't want me, please consider him. He's trying to set up on his own business, and he's a good guy. Just consider this a peace offering. Again, I'm sorry."

This was weird. Why would he bring this guy? He had to be nuts to think I'd let anyone associated with him back into my life.

"Here's his resume. I helped him because his English isn't that great." He handed me a creamy sheet of paper. "Come on." He gestured to Jorge, and both of them climbed into the van. Scott waved as they turned and drove down the drive. I clutched the paper, wrinkling it in my hand. I gasped. What was I doing? Why would I touch anything he'd hand me? I started to shake with fear. Then, I searched my feelings, had anything changed? Not that I could tell. I reached out with my magic. Was the paper imbued with a spell or a potion? I didn't feel anything except fury building.

Megan and Mr. Mittens slunk out of the woods and joined me at the back porch. I sat down and stared at the paper in my hands. It was indeed a resume with all of Jorge's building and restoration experience, nothing more. Why did I get all the strange ones? Why had Scott brought him by, and did he really expect me to hire him? I wadded the paper into a ball and clutched it in my hands.

"That was weird," Megan said as she sat next to me. "I couldn't hear it all, but Mr. Mittens filled me in. He really had the balls to ask you to take on a guy that worked for him? Is he nuts?"

I nodded, still stunned. "Yeah."

"Alrighty then."

I shook it off and stood. I walked into the house, tossing the paper in the recycle bin.

"What time are we meeting the werewolves?" I asked Megan, since she'd been the one coordinating with Luke.

"Luke said to be ready, he'd call once Sofia left."

"OK."

I stepped wearily into the house. I grabbed a glass and filled it with water from the fancy fridge and drank it.

Megan was watching me oddly. "He really did a number on you, didn't he?" she asked.

"Yup. And I let him." I rolled the cool glass over my forehead. "I knew better. After everything with Evan, I should have been more wary."

"You can't blame yourself. You were drugged or magicked or whatever. Not your fault."

"Doesn't stop me feeling like this."

"Yeah, I know. Sorry." She looked miserable. "I just hate seeing you like this. Look at all you've accomplished on your own." She waved at the house. "You discovered your magic and became a badass. You don't have any reason to feel bad."

Even though it shouldn't have, her speech buoyed me a little from the depression I felt coming on. She was right. It wasn't my fault, and I could take care of myself. I had friends now. True ones. Mr. Mittens, Megan, the Whelans, Brightfeather, Goch, and Gabe—as soon as I freed him. My old life was done. I didn't even need to look back at it. I could move forward.

I sat in the kitchen chair and finished my water. "Thanks, Megan." I put all of my love and gratitude for her into that simple phrase. She leaned over the chair and hugged me.

Her phone rang. She stood back up and pulled it from her back pocket. She looked at the screen. "It's go time," she said, then answered the phone. "Hey, Luke."

I couldn't hear the other side, but they didn't talk for very long. Megan's face was serious and angry. She hung up.

"There's a problem," she said. "We've gotta go now."

My heart accelerated. "What's wrong?"

"I'll tell you on the way, let's go."

I followed her out the door. Mr. Mittens jumped up on the balcony rail. "Are you coming?" I asked.

I do not have much power away from this land, he reminded me with a head shake.

"I know, but you are always welcome to be with me."

His chest puffed up a little, and I could see that my statement made him proud.

Be safe, pet.

I patted his head as I passed and headed down the porch stairs. "I will. See you soon."

I climbed in the passenger side, and Megan turned the car and headed down the drive.

Once we were on the way, I repeated my question. "What's wrong?"

"It appears that Sofia did have a plan for Gabe during her two-day trip. She encased Gabe in ice. Madison must have tried to stop her, because she is also frozen in a block of ice."

I gasped, involuntarily. "What?"

Megan shrugged. "That's what Luke said over the phone. He was in a panic. I said we'd get there as soon as possible."

"I don't know how to thaw anyone out safely!"

"Well, you have between here and Gabe's to think of something."

That sent me back down the rabbit hole of self-doubt. If Sofia froze Gabe, she must have a safe way to unfreeze him. I doubt she'd leave him like that forever. If she wanted him dead, there were easier, less obvious ways. I didn't think she wanted that though. In some sick way, she had a thing for him.

Good grief. I was a beginning magic user, not a powerful well-trained witch. How was I going to do this? I mulled it over, becoming more and more agitated as we drew closer. I had no way to contact Dana for help, calling my grandfather required the moon at its zenith and a ridiculous ritual. I didn't dare just try to melt them or set them on fire. I could kill them.

I guess I needed to assess the issue first. We pulled into Gabe's driveway and around to the back of the house where the parking area was. I climbed out. The Whelans were there, milling around the backyard. As we approached, I could see that the reason the Whelans were agitated. They were looking all around Madison who stood unmoving with a thin film of ice surrounding her.

I joined the family members. "When did this happen?"

Noah stepped forward. "Sometime in the last hour. It was her shift to watch Gabe. When we didn't get a report within thirty minutes, and no answer on her phone, Luke came out to check on her and found this." He gestured to Madison's frozen form.

"Gabe is inside."

I followed Noah into the house. Gabe stood frozen in place, leaning against the kitchen counter staring off into his adjoining living room. He was the same—frozen in place with a thin barrier of ice encasing him. Luke was staring at the Gabe statue, examining everything he could to find a way to thaw the two people.

I joined him in looking up close at Gabe. His eyes were staring straight ahead, but something was odd. I reached into my back pocket and flicked on my phone flashlight. Then, I shined the light in Gabe's eyes. Slowly, his pupils shrunk in response to the bright light directed at them.

"Did you see that?" I asked.

"Yeah," Luke said. His face inches from mine as he stared into Gabe's eyes.

"They're still alive and reacting, if very slowly."

"So, what do we do?" Luke asked. Noah moved closer to hear the answer.

"Umm, I don't know. I'm afraid if we thaw them too quickly, it'll hurt them somehow—burn them or something, and I don't know how dangerous that would be. If we do it too slowly, they might suffer from hypothermia. I just don't know!"

I started to panic, to breathe too fast, and my heart pounded. I didn't want to be responsible for this decision. I wasn't a medical professional or a competent magic user.

Luke put his hand on my shoulder. "We'll put our heads together, come on, let's go outside with everyone else."

I nodded, grateful, and followed the werewolves out to the statue of Madison. Once outside, I needed to determine if Madison was also reacting and alive in her case of ice.

"Has anyone noticed any reaction?" I asked the family standing around and studying her.

They shook their heads. I tried the light thing with Madison, but she was in the sun, and her pupils were already pinpricks. I ran back in the house and grabbed Gabe's jacket from a hook inside the back door. I put it over Madison's head and waited for one minute which I timed on my phone. After the minute ended, I yanked off the coat and studied her eyes. I breathed a sigh of relief. "Her pupils have expanded. She's alive," I announced.

The family seemed to sag in relief. That was the immediate concern, that she was alive in the ice. The second one was how to free her from it while keeping her unharmed.

Luke ran inside. We followed. He dug through the kitchen drawers and came out with one of those long stick lighters for candles, or barbecue grills. Before I could stop him, he held it up to Gabe's arm, clicked it on, and let the flame touch the thin barrier of ice. I gasped. He held it there long enough the thin ice should have melted, and the flame should have caught his sleeve on fire. But nothing happened.

"Regular fire doesn't do anything. It might have to be magic fire," Luke said.

Megan and the Whelan's all stared at me. I swallowed, the blood rushing out of my head. I swayed.

I stumbled back outside, sucking in air so I didn't pass out from the weight of the family's need to save their sister and daughter.

I stopped by Madison's frozen body.

Anna, the Whelans' mother, came over to me. She placed a comforting hand on my arm and looked me in the eye. "This is a lot of pressure, Brigid. We know. Whatever you decide, we'll support you." That was a brave thing for the girl's mother to say, but it added to the pressure instead of relieving it.

I smiled weakly. "I wish I had a book or guide that went with all of this, but I don't. Whatever decision we make, I'll have to live with it."

I explained the dilemma about either burning them or causing hypothermia. After much discussion, they decided that burning them would be best, because if we awakened Gabe, he could heal them both. Whereas hypothermia would be scarier if we couldn't get Gabe active and aware quickly. I nodded, still too terrified to try. I wished Mr. Mittens had come, his presence always reassured me and gave me confidence.

What I really needed was advice from someone with Fae magic like mine. Even though a witch had done this, she'd done it with my ice magic. I didn't know if that changed the use or how to undo it, but it had to factor in. I explained my reasoning to the Whelans.

When they didn't appear moved, I added. "I can call my grandfather at the moon's zenith."

"We don't know how safe it is to keep them in this state," Noah argued.

I looked at him and realized my hands were clasped together. I let them fall. "No, but Sofia wants Gabe alive and well, so I assume they'll be safe for two days at least. If I can wake them up tonight, we'll still have time to make plans with Gabe," I replied.

Noah stared at me for a second, and then the Whelans spoke amongst themselves while I waited with Megan.

Finally, they came back. "We can wait, it's probably safer if we have guidance from someone familiar with this magic," Noah said. Then he pointed to Michael and Luke. "Let's get Madison in the house, out of the sun in case that does anything weird to her or melts her too soon."

The boys picked up their frozen sister gently and placed her in the kitchen next to Gabe. I didn't notice any water or evidence the warmth from the house was melting Gabe, so maybe the magical ice would hold up to natural heat and sunlight as well as to flame. I didn't know. When Sofia had made an ice wall to block me from attacking her, I'd melted it with my fire magic without any effort. I didn't dare do that to people, but I was afraid that was what it would come down to.

Anna decided to stay and guard her daughter and Gabe, and the rest of the wolves, Megan, and I went back to the house to wait for the moonrise and another call to my grandfather for help. I hoped he was in a good mood.

Chapter Fourteen

Luke and the other Whelan's looked at me strangely when I explained the ridiculous ritual. When I googled when the moon would be at its zenith, it was early in the evening, 5:16 p.m. It would still be light. That would be a change. It also didn't give us much time to prepare. So, after I explained what would happen, I quickly gathered the supplies I needed and hurried out to the altar.

Megan decided to stay behind with the Whelans at my house. Mr. Mittens accompanied me because he insisted on "protecting" me from my own woods. It was a good idea since I still wasn't over the unicorn incident.

I set up the altar and danced my dance before I said the stupid rhyme. I felt better this time, and the movement didn't hurt. At the end of the chant, my grandfather, without a delay, appeared in a blaze of light. He wasn't dressed for war this time, but he was still grumpy.

"Why did you summon me?" he demanded, his voice thunderous in the still clearing.

"Forgive me, grandfather. I don't have any way to

contact you or Dana, and I have a pressing magical emergency," I said, nervously.

"Well, what is it, child? I cannot stay long," he answered and crossed his huge muscle-bound arms over his equally muscle hard torso.

Mr. Mittens jumped up on the altar and folded his tail neatly around his legs, watching with his luminous blue eyes. It started to mist. I shivered.

"Umm, the witch that stole my magic, used my ice to freeze two of my friends into statues." I opened my phone and showed him the pictures of Gabe and Madison encased in their thin veil of ice.

He held the phone with a frown, examined the device carefully—as though it was going to burn him—and finally looked at the photos. I flipped the page back and forth so he could view both victims.

"What is this clever device?" he asked.

"It's a smart phone. A small computer that allows me to make phone calls and access the internet. It also acts as a camera, and lots of other things."

"Phones when I was last here were simple machines," he intoned. "I do not understand computer?"

"Yes, phones have changed a lot in the last few years." I put the phone back in my pocket and looked up at him. I had no idea how to explain a computer, so I ignored that part of his statement. "What about my frozen friends? Is there a way to unfreeze them safely?"

"Yes, we should conclude our business quickly. I can explore the changes in this realm later. As for unfreezing them, there are two possibilities. You melt them with your fire magic, or you reverse your ice magic."

I opened my mouth to interrupt him and remind him I'd lost the ice magic, but he put up a hand to stop me. "I know the issues with your ice magic. The fire magic is a difficult one, as you'll have to be careful not to burn your friends. You will need to apply a thin layer of magical fire to the ice and melt it swiftly. As soon as the ice is gone, you should place your friends in a warm bath and bring their body temperatures up swiftly."

I cringed, terrified that I would either burn them or not get their core temperatures up in time. "Is there no other way?" I asked, hope flaring at his "reverse the ice magic" statement.

"If you wish to wait a day or two, I can have my mistress of magic attempt the task; however, I warn you that she will not be as worried about damage to their frail mortal shells as you will be."

That was the problem. At least I'd been on the right track, and I knew there was no other way out of this mess.

"Is that all, child?" he asked. I was surprised at how reasonable he was being after being summoned against his will.

"Grandfather, is there another way to contact you or Dana if I have a need? This way requires time, and some things are time sensitive."

He tilted his head in thought. "I will think on it. My mistress of magic will bring you the answer."

Without even a goodbye, he vanished in a flare of light. I sighed wearily. Mr. Mittens hadn't said anything, and I was surprised, although he and my grandfather had shared a quick glance, and perhaps a quick mental word.

"Did he say anything to you?" I asked him as we walked back to the house.

Nothing pertinent to the problem, he responded.

"Was it about me?"

It was…personal.

128

I looked at my cat. He didn't seem upset or worried, so maybe it had just been a greeting or catch up between friends. Maybe someday he would fill me in on his backstory and how he became trapped in this realm as my protector.

Suddenly, a thought came to me. I'd assumed that my grandfather and my cat were friends, maybe their relationship was different than that. "Are you friends with my grandfather?"

We are friendly, he answered or evaded. I wasn't sure, but his tone implied he didn't want to talk about it. I let it go. Not my focus at the moment. Now, I had to perform precise magic that could end in the maiming or death of one or both of my friends.

The house was full of nervous werewolves and Megan. They all waited impatiently to hear what the answer to our problem would be. I still wasn't sure what to do. Should I attempt to thaw them? Should I depend on Dana to show tomorrow morning and have her do it for me? Or just have her close to guide me? I couldn't decide, but when it came down to it, I didn't have to decide alone. I told them everything that my grandfather had said, including the choices we had—my magic fire, waiting for Sofia to do it when she showed up in two days, or waiting for Dana to show me tomorrow or the next day.

"Sofia is out," Luke said, and everyone agreed, including me.

"Yes," Noah agreed. "I think we should wait for the magic instructor."

"But, there's no guarantee she'll be here in time or be gentle or careful with people she doesn't know," Luke added.

Izzy nodded. "I agree. I think that Brigid should try. We know she'll be careful."

"But I'm a newbie!" I protested. "What if I burn them, or don't do it right and they freeze to death? Maybe we should wait for Dana, if you don't want her too, at least she could instruct me and guide me."

Megan jumped in. "No, she isn't human. How can you trust her? Plus, she might not get here until Sofia is back."

Even though I didn't think Dana would care about helping humans, she cared about pleasing my grandfather —and she'd been punctual so far. However, it sounded like my grandfather might have her tied up for a day. But she was still a risky choice. I explained my reasoning to the group.

Luke acknowledged us both with a tilt of his head. "I agree with Izzy, Brigid, I think you can do it. You'll be careful, even more so because you care about Gabe and Madison. And best of all, you can do it now."

Michael, Luke, and Izzy were onboard. I looked at Noah, desperate for him to nix the operation. It would be better if Dana did it. She may not care about them, but she was a master magic user. I shook my head.

"Fine, I trust Brigid as well," Noah said to his family. "Brigid, you have all of our faith."

My eyes flew open wide; I swallowed hard and looked at Megan. She gave me a sympathetic look. "I believe in you," she said.

I took a deep breath and let it out slowly. "OK. I'll try."

With nothing else to do but give it the old college try, we decided to go. Everyone filtered out, and we headed back to Gabe's where we'd see if I could unfreeze them.

Chapter Fifteen

I visualized what I would do, just as my grandfather had instructed. I'd need to have a tub waiting with warm water, towels, and maybe a car running in case we needed to get them to the ER as quickly as possible. I wasn't sure how I'd explain severe hypothermia when the weather was mild, but we'd cross that bridge if we came to it. I wavered between which one to attempt the thaw on first. If I thawed Madison first, I'd have the practice to work on Gabe, who was most important because he could heal her if something went wrong. However, maybe I should thaw Gabe first, so he'd be available if something went wrong with Madison.

Since I couldn't decide, I put it before everyone. The final consensus was to thaw Gabe first. He was the healer. He could heal himself and be ready for Madison once she thawed.

"Do you want to do it in the kitchen?" Megan asked me as we examined our two frozen friends.

I hadn't gotten that far in my plans.

"Hmmm, if we do it here, then we have to carry them

to the bath. Plus, there's a chance I'll burn down the house."

"We could do it in the bathroom and have the fire extinguishers ready," she suggested.

It was a good idea, so I nodded, and the werewolves picked up Gabe and carried him to the main floor bathroom—the only one in the house with a tub. We placed him in the middle of the floor so I could walk around him and filled the tub with room temperature water. If he was hypothermic, we'd need to gradually increase the temperature, otherwise he'd be in agony.

The bathroom could only hold Gabe, me, and two werewolves, and that was a little too chummy for me, but we needed those fire extinguishers on hand. The others waited outside the bathroom, all in various states of nervousness. If this didn't work, Madison would likely have to be thawed by Dana, and that unknown wasn't something they wanted to face.

With nothing left to delay me, I faced Gabe. "Please forgive me," I said to him, and then I closed my eyes, and gathered my will. Once I thought I was ready, I focused on my ring and called the fire. Grandfather said to do a fine even layer all at once. So that's what I told my fire to do. Once the ice melted off of his skin, we had to get him in the water. I could warm that gradually from the faucet, so hopefully, he'd be OK once we made it that far.

The fire came, and at first, it was too much. I scorched his bathroom tiles and ceiling, before I found the right balance. The ice evaporated. Or just plain disappeared. It was strange, when you melt ice, you expect water to be the next state of matter, but the ice didn't melt, it just went away. I knew it was gone when I smelled the burning of Gabe's clothing. I cut off my magic, and Luke and Noah

132

lowered him into the tub. He was still not responding. Hopefully, with the magical ice gone, he'd stir soon.

The water put out his steaming clothes. Two minutes passed, three…

I was beginning to get nervous I'd failed, and Gabe was dead, when he took a sharp intake of air and began to thrash.

"Gabe, it's Brigid! Calm down," I begged. It took him a moment to realize what was going on.

"Brigid?" he asked confused.

Ugh, he'd forgotten or been forced to forget again. I placed my hand on his head and undid the spell as I'd done once before. Again, it took a moment, then the memories came flooding back, and he realized who I was.

"Brigid!" he said again, recognition in his eyes. "What's going on?" He looked around, seeing the wolves, me, and finally himself in the bathtub, fully clothed. He lifted his arm, the water dripping from it. He began to shiver. I turned the water fully to hot and allowed the bath to gradually warm, letting water out as needed, until he indicated that he was warm.

I sighed with relief.

"How are you feeling?" I asked once the shakes had stopped.

"Better now. I'm warm, finally. I can't believe she encased me in ice."

"Yeah, me either. Unfortunately, you aren't the only one she did it to.

Gabe looked at me his eyebrows pushed together. "Who?" he asked, stunned.

"Madison Whelan. We had her watching the house. Well, all the Whelans have been taking turns, but it was on her watch. Somehow, either Madison confronted her, or

Sofia caught her and froze her as well. Once you're able to get out of the tub, we're going to thaw her as well. We figured it would be best to have a healer on hand."

"Yes, of course." He stood, the water falling off his clothes, and I handed him a towel. He wrapped himself in it and moved into his bedroom to change in privacy. He came out a few minutes later, his hair tousled, with dry clothes on. He had a bundle of wet clothes wrapped in his towel, which he tossed into his laundry room.

He couldn't avoid seeing Madison, still frozen in his kitchen. He examined her visually, then reached out a hand to press it against the ice.

"She's still alive," he said in wonder. "She's not fully frozen, everything is still functioning, only very slowly. Her heart is…ba…bump…ba…bump." He said each sound, taking several seconds for each, drawing out the sound of her extra slow heartbeat.

I watched, fascinated. "You can do that because of your healing ability?" I asked, although it was an obvious question.

"Yes. I can 'hear' all of her body sounds. She is still functioning, only in extreme slow motion."

I looked at her family, who were anxious to bring her back.

"OK, let's get her into the bathroom."

Her brothers picked her up and placed her gently in the spot where I'd thawed Gabe. The tub was still full, and I let some water out and refilled it until the water was lukewarm.

This time, I had the feel of how much fire to use to thaw the magical ice, and I did so. No fire extinguishers needed, and only a spot or two on her clothes that were scorched.

Once done, her brothers lowered her carefully into the tepid tub.

When she came to, it was with her hands flung forward screaming, "No!"

Luke knelt beside the tub and spoke to her until she realized where she was.

"What happened?" she asked, looking at all of us, her face a mask of confusion. "I was waiting for Sofia to leave, then…" She looked away, remembering. "Then I don't remember. She put her hands out, and I thought she was going to throw a nasty spell at me, and now I'm here." She used a hand to indicate the tub.

I nodded, and Luke took her hand. "She froze you in ice."

"Ice?" She shivered. "That explains why I'm so cold."

"I can fix that," I said and turned the heat all the way up, adding it to the tepid water already in the tub.

It took a few minutes before she indicated that she was warm, and we helped her out. Her mother took her into the spare bedroom, and she came out in dry clothes a few minutes later, her wet things in a reusable grocery bag. I drained the tub while we waited. We went out to Gabe's living room to talk about what to do next.

"What was she thinking, freezing you?" I asked. "She knows you'll be missed at the clinic!" I started off.

He shook his head. "I don't know. She's so worried I'll leave her or plot against her."

"And that's what we're going to do," Luke added.

Gabe smiled. "Yes, we are, but I need to call the clinic first."

Gabe found his phone, went into the kitchen, and made his call. From the sound of it, he was on call, and just checking in with a sorry excuse that his phone died, and he didn't notice. That was stupid—of course, he'd never be that irresponsible.

Once his call was done, he came in.

"Everything was fine, there hadn't been a call in, so it worked out. I can't imagine how I'd explain an entire weekend without being available when I'm on call. Sofia has gone too far."

I agreed, she'd been going too far for a long time. Freezing both of them, killing Craig, stealing my magic. It was all too far.

We settled back down on the living room furniture. Noah looked angry. That was a rare look for the new alpha. All of Craig's sons were happy, well-adjusted individuals, and it showed in their sunny smiles, warm greetings, and generally contented natures. Noah's grim face, tight lips, and the burning in his eyes was scary.

"What do you know of her plans?" Noah asked.

"Her plans are just what you think. She plans to capture Brigid and take the rest of her magic." Gabe stood and paced the large living room. "She hasn't spoken about all of her specifics, but she has plans for the next full moon, and she has members of the coven watching you..."—he gestured at me—"all the time. Even on your property."

I jerked. How? I wondered. I had Mr. Mittens, Brightfeather, and now Goch watching for intruders. That seemed nearly impossible. "How?" I murmured. But the sharp ears of the werewolves perked up. They all looked at me, which caught Gabe's attention.

"She hasn't said, but she is powerful. Perhaps some kind of concealment spell."

I hadn't considered that. I could do a kind of invisibility spell using my elemental magic, but who's to say there weren't other ways to do it. I knew nearly zero about witch magic, and even my teachers probably didn't know much more. We weren't witches.

"Oh," I said. "That makes sense. I wish I knew about witch magic. It would be helpful."

Gabe nodded. "I know about some, being the recipient of the nasty things more than once." He sighed.

I couldn't imagine how awful it would be to always be on the lookout for some witch coven or the other. Always looking over your shoulder, trying to stay off their radar. They always wanted him for what he could do—fill their magical wells. It was disgusting. If they'd only asked, he'd be willing, instead they had to control and twist everything with their evil little hands.

"Are all witches so…evil?" I mumbled. I wasn't thinking. I knew that comment would hurt Gabe. His ex had been a witch, and she'd done a real number on him.

Luckily, only the wolves heard, and when they looked at me, I waved it away as the rhetorical question it was. The answer was most of the time they were all evil. There might be a few out there with glowing pure souls, but not here. Here they were all involved in this plot. They'd already murdered for it and would stop at nothing until their goal was met—drain me completely of my magic and then kill me.

I lost the train of the conversation in my musings. When I came back to it, Noah was speaking.

"…with you."

"I don't know for sure, other than the obvious," Gabe said. "But she is acting like I'm her boyfriend to the coven and to the people at work. It's disgusting. I resist even under the spell."

I picked up on what they'd been talking about.

"Gabe, it's time to get out from under her control. We can't ask you to continue this…" I added.

"I want to leave. But I'm the best source of information right now. We'll be fighting her blind if I don't stay."

"Then we'll fight her blind," Luke replied.

The ache in my chest was starting to melt. We could do this. We could defeat her. Even if we didn't have inside information. I was getting more control with each lesson. I didn't know spell work or anything like that, but I had raw power, and I was gaining control with each attempt to work my magic.

"We have more allies now," I added. Although one dragon seemed to be a little thing despite his size.

They looked at me.

"Yes?" Noah asked. Confused.

"The other day…" I started and trailed off. How did one explain running into a dragon while on a nature walk? "I ran into a red snake, only it wasn't a snake, it was a dragon."

There was a collective gasp.

"Dragon?" Noah repeated.

"Yeah, a huge red dragon. His name is Goch. I think a dragon is a good ally, even if he's only a teenager and a little distractible. His heart is in the right place though." I was babbling. I'm sure none of that made sense to the group. I blushed.

"Dragon?" Luke repeated. I think they were a little stunned.

"Yes. A real live, fire-breathing dragon. Oh, and he's big. Did I say that already?"

"Yeah," Luke said.

"Where do you put a dragon?" Izzy asked. "If he's that big, how do you hide a bright red dragon?"

I shook my head. "Around anyone that isn't approved, he has to appear as a red snake. So, easy to hide in eight hundred acres of mostly wilderness."

She nodded. "OK."

Noah cleared his throat. I guess he'd snapped out of it. "A dragon is a great ally. We'll have to ask him if he has any kind of spell resistance."

That question got my mind swimming. Spell resistance?

"Is spell resistance a thing?" I asked.

Every head nodded.

"Do werewolves have spell resistance?" I know that Craig had succumbed to a spell, but it had taken a nasty fall for that to happen.

"Generally, we are resistant to a lot of things, unless we are weakened somehow. Like Dad was," Noah added quietly.

"I wonder if Brightfeather is as well," I said aloud, but it was just a passing thought. I figured my cat was, he'd taken down a lot of critters that should have killed him, and he'd prevailed. And during the fight with the witches, he'd come out unscathed. Something to ask all of my magical creatures.

"Please come with us, Gabe," I begged, although it caused my heart to race just to ask. I didn't know what I'd do if he refused. "You can stay in the house, or if that makes you uncomfortable, you can stay at the dairy in the house there."

All the Whelans also invited him to stay with them.

He looked at all of us, considering. Finally, he conceded with a sigh, "Yeah, this isn't working with Sofia. She isn't giving me enough information that living like this is viable. Freezing me and Madison, that's just taking it too far," he repeated.

"Yeah," I agreed.

He stood. "I'll pack a bag and lock up here. Brigid, I'll take you up on that offer."

A knot in my gut lessened. I'd been so worried—mainly about him being with Sofia but partly because of the thought of being rejected. Now, we just had to keep him free of her clutches while he was at work, but he'd be safe at home once I informed my guards what to look out for. At least, I had plenty of room.

Chapter Sixteen

Dana didn't care what day of the week it was. I didn't know if in the Faerie realm they even had a weekend. Or, for that matter, if they had equivalent days of the week. I also didn't dare ask her, no reason to make her grumpier if I was taking her weekends. She showed up bright and early, cleaned us out of pastries, and away we went to my "place of power." I wish I felt powerful. But my instincts were right, she'd have been here in time to save Gabe and Madison if we'd have waited.

Shockingly out of character for her, she'd actually engaged me in conversation for a few seconds. "Did your friends thaw properly?" she asked after we arrived at the waterfall.

"Yes, it went well," I replied.

She grunted in acknowledgment, another version of "adequate" I assumed.

She thrust an object at me.

"This will allow you to contact us in case of an emergency," she said. I took the object, and so I wouldn't annoy her, I placed it in the pocket of my jeans.

"How do I use it?" I asked.

"Hold it in your hand and focus on the recipient. In this case either myself or your Grandfather. Once the object lights up, you can speak your piece, and the message will be transmitted."

"OK, that seems easy."

"Yes, even you can't make a mistake using this." She sniffed.

At least she was consistent.

Since we'd already worked on a defensive magic with shadow, she taught me how to throw fireballs as an offensive weapon. I was better at this than the other things she had me do—at least at forming them. My throwing was another issue, but she didn't dwell on that, and we were done earlier than usual. She must have another pressing issue to let me get away with it. After she flashed away, I walked myself back to the house, Mr. Mittens trotted along in front of me, watching for threats.

"Do you have any magic resistance?" I asked since I'd been curious.

He stopped and threw a glance back at me. *Yes, I have some resistance here on this land.*

"Do you think that Brightfeather and Goch do as well?" I continued, filling the looming silence.

Most likely. Magical creatures usually have some kind of magical immunity based on their species, but for more specifics, you would need to ask them.

That made sense, so I nodded, although he couldn't see me, and we continued to walk. "What specific immunities do you have?" I asked after a moment or two.

Hmpf. His usual response if he were thinking or

annoyed. Probably annoyed, I was distracting him from his "patrol." *I am immune to most spells, although not to direct elemental attacks.*

"So, you could resist anything a witch threw at you, but not a Fae?"

I got the impression of a shrug in my head, so most likely, but not a perfect yes or no.

It depends on the strength of the attack, but most witch spells have no effect.

That was interesting. I was glad he was safe in this conflict I had with Sofia; I couldn't bear to see him sick or dying again. The spider bite still scared me when I thought of how close I came to losing him. In the short time I'd had him with me, I had grown extremely attached.

We continued to saunter back to the house, not in a great hurry. Gabe was at work, and although he was staying in the house, things had been if not strained, then uncomfortable. He'd had to flee his home and come stay with me and Megan, knowing that he'd been acting as Sofia's boytoy for a short time. He had suffered trauma and had to face Sofia once she returned. All not his fault.

I breathed out a loud sigh, and Mr. Mittens glanced my way. *What is the matter, pet?*

I didn't know how to put all my frustrations into words, but the cause of everything was easy to identify. "Sofia."

Ah. Yes, she is a problem. If she comes back to this property, I will consider her a creature to be destroyed, he said matter-of-factly.

"Me too." I tripped over a rough patch on the trail. He waited until I was steady, and we continued our walk. "Unfortunately, if it were that easy, we would have already eliminated her."

Yes. It is regretful.

I agreed with that as we quickly approached the house.

"Oh, I almost forgot. Gabe told us that we are being watched by coven members on this property."

Mr. Mittens stopped short, and I almost ran into him. His tail whipped from side to side in irritation.

How is this possible? he asked with a growl.

"Gabe said they are using concealment spells to hide themselves from us."

Mr. Mittens's growl grew louder as if he were Splintercat size. *I'll be back, pet.*

I chuckled at his unintended Schwarzenegger impression and watched him fondly as he disappeared into the trees. I wondered what he was going to do. Impulsively, I bellowed after him, "Bring them *alive* for questioning."

Megan was on the phone when I entered the kitchen through the back door. "Yeah, that works, see you then."

I opened the fridge to find something to drink. I pulled out a can of Diet Coke and popped the top open. "What was that about?"

"We have a handyman coming, I called one from your list. He's going to check out the little things we need done here and look at the dairy house as well." She beamed with pride.

"Cool, I can check that off. Did you find out what licenses and things we need to open the B&B?"

"Yup, they've been sent to your email, we are on our way!"

"That's great. I'll look at them after I shower and clean up."

I climbed into my shower—I had to say my bathroom was my favorite place in the house—and cleaned up, scrubbing away the sweat and effort learning magic cost.

Once out, I retrieved my laptop and looked at the items we needed to complete before opening. The list was daunting but exciting in a way. This new project was the first thing besides restoring the house that filled me with anticipation. How would the B&B do? Would the supernatural community respond well to the idea? Were there others like it in the world, and probably the most anxiety causing thought, how would I advertise?

Megan was going to use her considerable computer know-how to see if she could locate other businesses that catered to the supernatural community. They had to exist. I couldn't be the first one to come up with the idea.

Before I took a deep dive into my computer, I heard Mr. Mittens in my mind.

I have one for you, pet, and yes, it is alive…

Well, shit.

"Megan!" I said, maybe louder than I intended.

"Yeah, what's wrong?" She looked up from her computer with a start. Mr. Mittens must have just sent that message to me.

"We need to meet Mr. Mittens outside."

She finished typing a few words and closed the laptop, following me out the door. In the protected gravel drive behind the house, Mr. Mittens stood with a large Splintercat paw pressed on the chest of a man dressed in camouflage. The man was writhing around, trying to escape, but it appeared my cat held him down with little effort. I shivered. At least the witch was still alive.

Megan looked at me and crossed her arms. "He's one of them, isn't he?" she asked. "A witch."

I nodded. Her face darkened with emotion.

We approached until we were looking down on him. He stilled.

"What are you going to do to me?" he asked, his voice cracking.

I looked at Megan, and then my cat. "It depends."

Mr. Mittens growled, and I saw the paw on the witch's chest flex, and the claws extend enough to just puncture the skin. The man tensed, then thrashed around again.

"OK, OK, I'll do anything!" he gasped.

"How many of you are watching my place?"

"Just me. I swear!"

"So, you come one at a time, or does it vary?"

Mr. Mittens extended his claws a millimeter more. The witch froze and drew in a sharp intake of breath. "It varies!"

"Continue…"

"We have up to three at a time. This is just in the middle of the day when everyone is at work."

"How are you hiding yourselves from me and my protector?" This time my voice was hard, and I had changed from crossed arms to hands on hips—my power move.

"We have a concealment spell. Sofia designed it."

I looked at Megan and Mr. Mittens as though I were considering their input.

It is true; the witch was concealed. Should I kill him now? Mr. Mittens asked.

I addressed the witch, "Is that all or should I let my cat kill you? He's hungry."

"No, no, ummm, Sofia, she's got a plan to take more of your magic!" he stammered out.

I waved a hand at Mr. Mittens, and he retracted his claws. "Tell me more."

"She'll kill me," he whispered.

I used my earth magic and had the ground move until he sunk slightly into it. His legs, bottom, and part of his chest were half covered.

"Wait!" he yelled.

"You don't think that I will kill you? Or my cat? Foolish." I released the earth, and he was lying on top of it again. Mr. Mittens licked his chops and dipped his head, his eyes lighting up with his intent.

"Everyone always discounts me," Megan said with a pout and lifted my best, eight-inch, kitchen filet knife.

My eyes flew open when I looked at her. I had discounted her as being the kind one. I shouldn't have. She knew this was deadly serious.

I nodded. "Sorry, I shouldn't have forgotten to mention you." Apparently, she wasn't only my ride or die friend, but also my ride and kill friend.

She smirked. "That's right."

"So, what else do you have to tell us?" I really didn't know what to do with him when we were done, I guess I'd let Mr. Mittens decide, although that was the witch's death sentence, but I couldn't let him go. Or could I? If he went back, maybe he'd terrify the others into leaving me alone. Of course, if he said anything Sofia would probably kill him, but at least that would be off my conscience.

He reached for his pocket. Mr. Mittens growled, and his claws extended again.

"I have a paper with the spell and the schedule, but it's in my pocket," he said.

I nodded at Mr. Mittens, and he allowed the witch to reach into his pocket. He pulled out a folded piece of notebook paper, and he reached up so I could take it.

I opened the paper, and sure enough, there was a handwritten schedule with a simple spell. "Sofia can't use a spreadsheet?" I asked, incredulous.

"She doesn't let us write things down, usually, evidence you know, but I kept forgetting my rotation."

"What about her plans to steal my magic?" I continued.

"I just know she has plans, but I'm not in her inner circle. I don't know what they are—I swear!"

I was disappointed; we already knew she had a plan from Gabe. I looked at the fear in his eyes and didn't think there was much more the witch could tell us. So, I gestured for Mr. Mittens to let him go. He growled but took his paw off the man's chest.

"I c-can go?" he stammered.

"Yes, you will leave my property. If we ever see you again, or you tell the other witches I know about the rotation, I'll let my cat eat you on sight."

He brushed himself off and bolted back to the trees, probably to wherever he had parked. Hopefully, he found his way quickly because as soon as I released Mr. Mittens, I doubted he'd get a second chance at escape.

"You caught him quickly," I remarked to my cat as he transformed once more into his Ragdoll form.

Hmpf. It was easy once I knew they were using a spell, he said with disdain.

"Have you talked to Brightfeather or Goch about the witches?" I asked.

Yes, they are aware and will be more vigilant, he replied.

"Thank you."

He nodded and strolled away to do whatever he did—I hoped it wasn't eating a stupid witch.

Chapter Seventeen

Gabe came in with another load of his things. I'd put him in a finished room on the second floor. He was still uncomfortable with me, and I didn't know how to make it right. I followed him upstairs.

"Are you OK?" I asked, as he put his bag on the floor.

He looked at me and smiled uncertainly. "I feel like we just barely restarted our relationship, and then I cheated on you."

That's what I thought it was. "Gabe, I don't blame you. You were under her spell. I blame her." I looked him straight in the eyes. "If you want to see what we can be to one another, I'm still willing. You remember what I went through with Scott and the love potion? You didn't blame me. This is worse. Not your fault, and I don't blame you at all. There is zero to forgive. I know your heart, you're caring, loving, and giving. I know you would never have done this under your own will. I truly blame her. She's evil. You are not. Please believe that. Let's put this behind us."

"I also know how you feel about cheating. After your

149

husband…" He trailed off, his eyes intent on my face, trying to read any insincerity there.

"You didn't cheat. You didn't do anything wrong. You were spelled. You need to quit putting blame on yourself," I answered firmly, making sure I made constant eye contact, so he knew I was telling the truth.

He looked at me for a few moments more, then he nodded, and let out a breath. "Thanks, Brigid. None of this has been fair to you. You are too good."

I huffed. "I'm not good. I just threatened a witch with death by cat earlier today."

He laughed. "I'd have liked to see that."

"Yeah, too bad it wasn't Sofia."

His face darkened.

"Sorry, shouldn't have brought her up," I apologized.

He nodded. "It's OK, I'm still…" He waved a hand, but I understood. "So, was it a coven member spying?" He changed the subject.

"Yup, we didn't get specifics out of him, he told us he wasn't in her inner circle, but we have this." I pulled the paper with the names and rotation schedule out of my pocket and handed it to him. "You probably know more of these people than I do. Maybe you can identify if any of them are working at the clinic?"

He studied the paper for a few moments, his frown deepening. "That bitch," he whispered finally, almost so quiet I didn't hear him.

"What's wrong?"

He pointed to a name. "This woman is one of my medical assistants. This is how Sofia is always one step ahead of me."

"I'm sorry," I said.

He shook his head. "I'm taking care of this one, right now."

He took out his phone.

"I'll give you some privacy," I said and began to walk out of the room.

"You don't need to leave; this will only take a moment." He manipulated the phone and put it up to his ear. "This is Dr. Ambrose," he said. "Can you connect me with Sierra Curtis, please?"

There was a pause for a few moments. His hand was tense on the phone, his face grim. "Sierra? This is Dr. Ambrose. I know you've been spying for the coven. I want you out of my office. If you transfer, I will give you a good word, if you don't I'll fire you. Decide." He hung up. I could hear a protest on the other side before he ended the call.

I felt a momentary twinge for the hapless MA, but it only lasted a second. She'd spied for Sofia. She was probably on my land during the ceremony to steal my magic, and she'd certainly not offered up any medical services after my beating, so I shoved any sympathy down where it belonged.

"Good riddance," he said, his voice hard. He was one of the sweetest people I knew. So, having him this upset just cemented that my reaction to the witch earlier was warranted. I nodded.

He pointed to several other names he recognized, and he told me what businesses they worked at. There were a few more that were at the clinic, but no one else that worked directly with him. Who could believe that the evil witches in the coven would work in jobs that served people? It was so out of character. I wondered again if all witches were truly evil.

I had to let it go. The witches in the local coven, except for those too weak to use magic, were evil. They'd tried to kill me and my allies. They'd enslaved Gabe. I had to remember that. I told him that the Whelans had a more complete list of suspected coven members, and he nodded.

Time to up the protection on all eight hundred acres with three humans, a Splintercat, a griffin, and a dragon. That was a lot of area to cover. However, if the witches were smart, they were mainly watching the house, so I needed my protectors literally closer to home. Time to call a meeting.

"Gabe, I'm going to call a meeting. Do you want to join?"

"Sure," he said uncertainly, probably not knowing what I was talking about.

I smiled. "Come on." I put out a mental call to my protectors and led Gabe down to the kitchen and out the back door. We picked up Megan along the way and sat on the steps while we waited for the others to arrive.

Mr. Mittens was first. He probably hadn't gotten too far away after the witch, or he was patrolling around the house looking for more of them. Brightfeather and Goch were close behind, flying in. I'd given Goch permission to show his true form around Gabe, and he was grateful. Luckily, there was a large enough patch of tree free gravel back here from all the construction activity where he could land and stand comfortably.

"Wow," I heard Megan murmur. She hadn't met Goch yet and was still living in her fantasy of being a dragon rider. Frankly, dragon riding looked like it would be difficult, and require lots of muscle from all the jerking around that taking off, landing, and flying caused from what I'd observed of Goch's movement. Brightfeather was much smoother and more graceful. Although, Goch was young and would probably improve with age.

Goch's bright red coloring was flashy though and impressive upon first sight. I wondered if he could be seen from the road when he flew in. I'd have to ask him.

"Goch, how do people not see you flying?"

He lowered his head down to my level, which was nice, but horribly intimidating. *Dragons have magic that conceals us when we fly. That's why we are mostly just myths to most humans.*

"But I can see you."

You are in the know. The magic doesn't work well when people truly believe or have real knowledge of us.

"Huh," I replied.

Megan hung on every word. "How old are you Goch?" she asked. I was curious as well. So, we both waited for him to answer.

I know I'm young, but I hope that doesn't mean you won't let me help, he replied.

"That's not why I asked," Megan replied. "I am just curious. I don't know anything about dragons. I have no idea how long you live."

Goch looked abashed, which was interesting since he was already red in coloration, and didn't blush, his expression changed minutely, and he looked away slightly. *I am one hundred and thirty years old. Dragons can live for several thousand years. I know that I am young, but I am fierce!* He showed his impressive teeth. They were as long as a person and brutally sharp.

I gulped.

"You are the fiercest dragon we know," I reassured him. He appeared to preen a little, his eyes lighting up and his mouth curving slightly upward in a draconic grin.

Brightfeather also added her approval, and I continued with the meeting.

"Thank you, friends, for coming. I just wanted to let you all know that the witches are still spying, and they are using a concealment spell. They are watching me specifically, so if you are looking for them, I feel like they will be concentrated near the house. If you wouldn't mind checking it out on your daily sweeps, I'd appreciate it. Mr. Mittens…" I waved a hand at him, and he straightened up taller in his seated position. "Caught a witch earlier today. We discovered that they have a rotation to watch me here on my land. We have the list, so we know about how many witches will be here and when. Also, we do know for sure that she has a plan to capture me and take more of my magic. She'll be back in town tomorrow, so we should be prepared since we don't know when or what her plan entails."

My allies nodded grimly, and I knew they understood.

We are happy to help, mistress, Brightfeather said.

Goch also acknowledged that he would help.

"You can report to Mr. Mittens. Thank you, friends! Is there anything I can do to help you?" I asked.

Goch and Brightfeather were fine, but Mr. Mittens grumbled, *You can stay inside, my pet, and quit wandering around.*

I leaned down and scratched behind his ears. "You know I can't always do that. But I know you are just worried for me."

He purred. *I want you safe, my pet.* His face turned up to me, his eyes half shut, and he rubbed against my leg.

Warmth filled me at his words, and I ran a hand over his soft cottony fur.

Ok, here we go, I thought. Time to plan faster and harder than Sofia and have something ready this time around. I knew what ceremony she had to perform, she'd done it before, I knew when, same as before, and I knew where. I assumed she'd still do it at my altar in my woods—my magic was strong here, and she wanted it.

We had approximately one more week to go before the next full moon. And this time, I didn't want to be helpless and without my allies.

"We need to set a trap this time," I said to my companions. "And we'll have to set it by the altar. That's where she's going to attempt to strip my magic. Can you all search around that area to see if she's set anything up?"

They nodded and left.

I turned to Gabe and Megan. "She has to be looking for the missing pieces of my magic I'm still looking for as well. We need to find them first. So, that's our first step. I'm still missing air; it will have swirly markings. I guess any of them can be in the shape of a necklace, ring, or bracelet. Aether will be quartz stones, reality is unknown, and time will be represented by some kind of clock, so a watch or something similar. I've searched the inside of the house, the rest is either outside or in the woods."

I looked thoughtfully at the house. Just then, I heard a vehicle coming up my drive. I stiffened, and Gabe's face grew dark. Who was it now? Scott back to thrust more workers at me? Another witch trying to spy on me? That was dumb. They'd have to be sneakier than coming up a gravel driveway.

A white work truck with "Whelan Restoration" drove around the house and into the back parking area. I relaxed when I saw Luke and Izzy in the truck.

"Hi, guys!" I greeted them brightly, happy for their company and help searching.

Frankly, Luke was probably here to see Megan, but it was nice to have Izzy around.

We were becoming friends, and I liked to be around her.

Megan smiled at Luke, who came over and stood by her.

"What's up?" I asked.

Luke shrugged. "Just thought we'd come by and check on everything. Especially since there could be witches hiding and wandering around. Thought you might like a wolf or two to check."

"That'd be great. We'd love it. Actually, Mr. Mittens brought us a fine specimen earlier."

Luke started, and Izzy frowned with dismay. "What?" she asked, surprised.

"He took our comments about them being concealed to heart and flushed out a witch. We got a copy of their rotation plans and of the concealment spell and sent him on his way."

"Wow," Izzy said.

"Right now, we were going to start a search for the rest of my magic while we know there aren't any witches watching. If we can get it all first, we'll be better prepared for the next full moon."

"You think that's when she's going to try again?" Luke asked.

"I do." I had nothing to prove it but a gut feeling, but I'd been learning to trust that more and more.

"We'll help," Luke volunteered, and Izzy nodded.

"Cool, thanks."

Since this was as important as stopping Sofia, making sure I was completely armed, we spread out and started with the exterior of the house. Since Luke had the company truck—and it had tools, ladders, and scaffolding inside—he pulled out a ladder.

"I'll start with the roof," he said, and carried the ladder to the porch roof, where he could easily access the rest.

The rest of us spread out to cover the main floor porch and the patch of garden where I'd found the gris gris bag.

I don't know why I hadn't asked for help before now. I guess before the incident with the witches, I hadn't been serious enough about it, and then I'd been hurt and worried about Gabe, but it was time to drive the stakes up a notch. Fully magicked was how I could outpower Sofia and her coven.

I used my inherent magic, as Dana and my cat called it, and sent a call to my magic, to the jewelry that contained it, and I asked it to come to me, to show itself to me and my friends. I stood next to the house by the roses, arms wide, face to the sun, and let my magic pull the other parts of me home. When I opened my eyes, I saw a glint next to the house behind the roses. I was drawn to it, so I made my way through the rose garden.

Once I was near, I bent over, the glint was gone, but the pull was there. I reached out to the siding on the house, recently recovered with shiny new paint. So odd that the workers who'd been looking hadn't seen this. A single silver thread peeked out, I tugged on it, and a small velvet bag followed. I opened the bag, which was dusty, and partly painted, and out tumbled a ring into my hand. I gasped. It was a strange stone. When I gazed into it, I could see what felt like the universe, but a quick glance showed that instead it was a simple glowing blue jewel, and nothing more. Unable to resist the pull to study it more, I slipped it on my finger, and a wave of heat and longing for the unknown swept over me. I shivered and pulled my arms around myself. Reality. That was the piece. I hadn't known what the jewelry would look like, but when I gazed on it and re-integrated it, I knew.

The experience was eerie—that was the only word that came to me. Eerie. I had no idea what *reality* magic did, but it had an *immensity*, an ancient *pull*, to it that I had no idea what to do with. I took a deep breath, trying to steady myself, and leaned against the house, its solid realness re-attaching me to the now and the moment and the whatever that made this place what it was.

I cleared my throat after a moment and found I could speak. "I found one!" I yelled, and Izzy came around the house to give me a thumbs up.

"Any luck?" I asked her.

She shook her head. "I'm going to try the crawl space," she said.

"Really? It's dirty and there are spiders," I replied. I'd been a little weird about spiders since the soul spider incident.

"I've done worse," she said and smiled. Then, she took off her jacket, rolled up her sleeves, and headed for the small door hidden under the porch that led to the crawl space.

"Good luck," I called after her, and she waved briefly before disappearing into the gloom under the porch. I checked on Megan and Luke, but they were intently looking, and I didn't want to disturb them. I tried my call again, but something about finding the last artifact was keeping me distracted, and I couldn't connect like I'd done before. I went to the kitchen and made some sandwiches and drinks. I could be a good hostess, while everyone was working so hard to help me.

Just as I was finishing, I heard a call and rushed out. Luke was coming down the ladder. Once on the ground, he held up a necklace of quartz stones. It glittered and shot sparkles in the sunlight, and I clasped my hands together. Two pieces of magic in one day! Why hadn't I asked for help before?

Quartz, this must be Aether. Whatever that meant or did, but I gazed at the stones as my magic called to me to take it into myself. Luke watched my eyes and realized that I couldn't be in its presence for long without trying to pull the magic back inside of myself.

He held out the necklace, and I kept myself from snatching it, barely. I held it briefly until the compulsion was too much, then I slipped it over my head. The necklace flashed, and a light citrus scent wafted over me, and the feel of a sunny day breezed through me. Aether had a light touch which I was grateful for, especially since fire had been brutal.

"Ah," I sighed out.

Luke looked at me strangely. "What does it feel like? Reintegrating your magic like that?"

I looked at him. "Why, what did you see?"

He shrugged. "I saw a flash, and then your expression appeared...blissful, I guess is the only way to describe it."

"Yes, this one was blissful. They're all different. Each one has given a different sensation. Some have been unpleasant, but this one was light and easy."

"Interesting."

I nodded but felt slightly embarrassed. My cheeks warmed.

"I made sandwiches, if you're hungry," I said, changing the subject.

"Sure, I can eat. You'll find that offering food to werewolves is always welcome. We're usually hungry." He winked.

I laughed. "Anytime, I'm not much of a cook, but I can manage the basics."

He went inside and came back with a plate that had two sandwiches, a pile of chips, and a Coke.

I left him eating and went to gather up everyone for a break. I grabbed Megan and waved at Gabe to come in and sent them to the kitchen. I yelled for Izzy under the porch, and she called back, "Just a minute, I think I found something."

My heart sped up a beat. Three pieces of magic in one day? That would be the record. I'd be only one short if that happened, minus the ice magic Sofia had stolen, of course.

"Come under here, I can't quite reach it. You have longer arms."

I shuddered. After running into the soul spider, I had no desire to go where spiders lived, but it was for my magic, and that was more important than my newly acquired arachnophobia. I sighed and crawled under the porch and into the dark underbelly of my house. I could see where Izzy had crawled. The dust was disturbed, and I could see her light up ahead. There was more headspace under here than I'd imagined when she'd first crawled through the door. I could almost stand, or at least crouch down without hitting my head on the supports that held up my house.

She was looking at me and waving for me to hurry. She seemed excited. I wondered why. If it were a piece of jewelry, then she should react, but there was more excitement than that.

I crawled up and knelt next to her. "What is it?" I asked, because I didn't see anything at first.

"Oh, sorry." She pointed her light back into a hole

between supports. About three feet back, I could see what looked like a metal cigar box. I was only an inch or two taller than Izzy, so I wasn't sure I could reach it either. There was also no guarantee that a piece of my magic was in there either, because the box looked older than me by a lot. If my magic had been stored here at the same time as the box, it would be older than me, so nothing but a red herring.

Plus, I didn't want to stick my arm in a spider hole. I was still getting over the last one. My whole being was yelling *ick*.

But the box called to me. I was drawn to it as surely as if it did contain…*something*.

I reached my arm in, fighting the desire to run, strip off my clothes, and brush out my hair. I grazed the edge of it with my middle finger, but it was out of my reach.

"I can't reach it," I grumbled.

"Uh!" Izzy exclaimed. "We'll have to find a stick or something. I don't think my brother's meaty hands can fit. I'll be right back."

She crawled around me and headed out. I shivered and felt the desire to flee the spider infested crawlspace, but I held it together for the few seconds she was gone. She came back, finally, with one of those grabber things that short people need to reach the top shelves of tall cabinetry. I'd forgotten I had one of those in my kitchen. Vaulted ceilings were lovely, but they made it hard to reach my extended cabinets.

"That'll work," I said, and made room for her to shove the grabber in and grasp the box.

She handed me the flashlight. "Hold this!" I obeyed and held it so she could see the box and reach into the hole to pull it out.

I heard the grabber clink as it grasped the tin box, and the rasp as she pulled it out of the tight hole it was in. Finally, it lay between us, mysterious and old.

"Well?" she asked. "Open it."

"Me?"

"Yeah, your house, your box, your magic," she said.

I nodded. Of course, I was being silly. It was all of those things, maybe.

I reached out a hand. The box zinged under my fingers, and I snatched them back. There had to be a piece of my magic within. I opened it. Inside were a bunch of old photos. Photos of my family from when I was a small child. Probably near the time my magic had been taken. I shone the flashlight on them, and tears welled up. There was my grandmother. I hadn't realized I looked like her. In her nineties, she looked nearer my current age. She was smiling, and her auburn hair was falling around her face in waves, her bright blue eyes laughing. I'd thought she was so old then. Ha.

Then my mother and father gazing on me with love. I clutched the photos to my heart. I hadn't had many. I guess because they were still here at the house, and my heart swelled with love for my dead family. I pulled them all out and carefully laid them on my lap. The last item was a pocket watch. Time. It had to be. I held its silver case in my hand. Then, because I didn't know how to wear it to activate the magic, I opened the lid, and the timepiece was exposed for a moment. Then in a flash, it disappeared into my skin. My body buzzed with energy. It was the most invigorating feeling I'd ever had. I wanted to run, jump, laugh, and fling my hands to the sky.

I must have laughed out loud, because Izzy looked at me oddly.

"Time is a rush," I said, and she probably thought I'd gone over the edge.

We crawled out from under the house.

By then, the rush had worn off. I sighed, and we went into the house to eat.

Chapter Eighteen

The next day, Sofia was supposed to be back. We weren't sure when exactly, so I went to my lesson. I let Dana know I'd acquired Reality, Aether, and Time. She gave me an odd look when I asked her what they did. I sort of got Time, that one seemed obvious, but I didn't have a clue about the others.

"Reality," she said. "Is many things, but most importantly, it will allow you to walk the realms."

"Realm walk?" I asked, excitedly. That meant I could go visit the Fae realm and see my grandfather and how he lived. I was going to go visit too, once this conflict with Sofia was over. I could also go to Mr. Mittens's home realm. I'd been curious about it, since he was so closed- mouthed about his origins.

"Focus." She snapped her long extra jointed fingers in front of my nose.

I jerked my head back.

She appeared to be in a horrible mood.

"Yes, well. Realm walking is dangerous and not important right now. First, we must master the magic you need for the witches. That is my task to teach you. Xrsrphn can teach you to realm walk on your own time."

I nodded. She scared me more than a little, so I didn't argue. I was still dying to know what Aether was, but I supposed it could wait for another day. I had it and that was the most important thing. I was starting to feel whole for once and my magic less wounded.

She declared me adequate with fire, water, and shadow, and now we were working on light. Frankly, water, shadow, and light seemed like small potatoes next to Sofia. I thought we should be working on lightning, since that was my big scary power. At least it scared me.

"You're not paying attention," she yelled.

I wasn't, so I concentrated. My mind was with my friends and the weak plan we had to bring Sofia down in a few days when the moon was full once more.

I wove the light again. This time I kept my mind on it, and she declared me adequate and flashed away. I wondered if I would flash once I learned to realm walk. The first time my grandfather had appeared, there was a huge flash of light and a concussive force. That hadn't happened since, so I imagined he'd done that on purpose since he was pissed I'd summoned him.

Mr. Mittens met me at the spring, and we walked back to the house together. He, watching for intruders, and me, lost in thought over our coming conflict with the coven.

We made it back without any interruptions. We were going to meet with the werewolves later, since they were staking out Sofia and trying to figure out her plans. The coven must have already told her about Gabe, since he'd blatantly told off the coven MA from his office. I was sure she wasn't going to let him go without a fight.

He was at work. I had to trust he was safe in public at his own office. Even she'd not dared mess with his schedule too much. He was well-known and liked in town. The handsome, local boy, who came back to serve his community. No way she could interfere with that.

Megan was holding down the fort. The handyman she'd hired had begun the finish work we still needed done on the house. I was letting her take point, since we never knew how long my lessons with Dana would take every day. Megan was competent, so I wasn't worried.

When I came in, I heard the welcome sound of construction work from above, and Megan was on the phone and the computer at the same time. I was glad I'd hired her, not that there was a chance I wasn't going to. She was taking up all the slack and was going to get this business up and running while I was lacking in time.

I caught the tail end of her conversation as I walked in and realized she was talking to Luke. My heart warmed a little for my friend. She and Luke deserved happiness. I sure hoped they could make this thing between them work.

She hung up.

"Luke and Megan sitting in a tree…"

She rolled her eyes. "Grow up, Bridge."

I laughed. "I couldn't help it; you should see your gooey eyes when you talk to him on the phone."

"Well, he's pretty dreamy, you know." She smirked. "Besides, I'd like to cover him in gooey chocolate."

I laughed. "I bet."

A couple of sharp bangs came from upstairs.

"So, the handyman showed?" I asked.

"Yup, only it's a handywoman," she replied.

"Really? That's cool. What happened to the other guy?"

She shrugged. "He couldn't do the job, backed out. The

handywoman has good references and was willing to take on this rather large project, so we are grateful to have her."

"Yes, we are," I affirmed. Even Megan didn't know how grateful. From the beginning, my main goal was getting this house done. Now, I had the additional goal of having it ready to open as a B&B before spring.

"So, what did Luke say about Sofia. Is she back?"

"Oh, yeah, she's back, and apparently, she's raging. That witch you sent back to her?"

I nodded.

"Well, the Whelans aren't sure what is happening to him, but he's locked up in the coven's warehouse, and the coven are all heading there tonight to decide his fate."

I shivered. I knew this would happen when I released him. I figured Sofia would do something awful, but at the same time, I wanted the coven to be frightened of us as well. Any doubt we could throw their way had to be good for our side.

"If they are busy infighting, maybe they'll forget about me."

"You wish."

I nodded. It was a stretch. I still knew she was coming for me, and it would be in just three more days. Somehow, I had to make sure that all of us were ready.

"The Whelans can't get inside to check. The witches know about them and are watching for them. Luke said there's a ward on the warehouse," Megan continued.

"Well, that sucks." I sat at the table.

"Yeah, I was kind of wondering if the ward is just against magical types, and if I could sncak in," she said quickly, almost flippantly.

"I don't know. That's too dangerous, Megan. I'm not sure about that."

"No one knows who I am, if I get caught, I'll just say I was lost or something." Her jaw was set, and I knew she'd already decided she was going to try.

I stood up and put my hands on the table.

"So, you're going to do it, anyway? Is that what I'm hearing?" I said, my voice a little too high and loud as panic set in.

"You know me so well. Come on, you can be my backup."

"Not if I can't get through the ward."

She smiled at me. "Luke says if I can get inside, it's possible I can bring the ward down. Then, I'll have you and the werewolves as backup."

Damn Luke, I was gonna strangle him.

"How?" I put my hands on my hips, this sounded like a ruse to get me off her back.

She smirked. "Simple. I just need to break the circle. It's a requirement of a witch ward."

I huffed at her. "Do you know where the circle is? What if it's painted on? What if it's guarded?"

She frowned; she hadn't thought that through. Then, she shrugged.

"We'll cross that bridge when we come to it."

"You're going to get yourself killed or sacrificed or something. The witches aren't playing." I started to pace.

"It'll be fine, Bridge, I have faith in you and Luke's family to get me back safely." Her tone was matter of fact. She didn't even act scared.

I wasn't going to win; she was determined. "When?"

She looked at her phone. "Two hours. I'm waiting for Luke to be ready."

I threw up my hands and called my cat. I needed his

advice on breaking witch spells. He probably couldn't help, but he knew more than me.

"And Luke is OK with this plan?"

She lifted her hand and waved it back and forth to indicate so-so.

"Hmpf." Now, I sounded like Mr. Mittens.

Mr. Mittens came around the corner, just like a regular house cat on his own agenda. *You rang?*

I wanted to keep my mad going, but that made me giggle. I remember I would curl up in a chair with him when I was very small, and we'd watch reruns of *The Addams Family*. Apparently, he remembered too.

Megan must have heard him as well because she rolled her eyes. My cat was becoming more ridiculous by the day. He had a better sense of humor than I had first thought though.

"Yes," I said to him. "Megan is going to go crash the witches party at their coven's warehouse. It's warded, apparently. Do you know anything about breaking a witches' ward?"

I thought back to when they'd captured me and kept me bound and contained under a ward. That had been an active working though, so I didn't know if they were the same. He couldn't get through that one, but several witches had been chanting and using magic to hold it against him, Brightfeather, and the wolf pack. Maybe a passive working would be easier to break.

Hmpf. I am not a witch or a Fae, he grumbled.

I sighed. "I know, Mr. Mittens, but you were the protector of a witch, and you've seen more magic than I have. I was just hoping you'd have more information than I do."

He cocked his head and blinked his enormous peri-winkle blue eyes at me. *I do.*

That was an understatement; he was somewhere around two hundred years old.

"About wards and witches?" I prompted.

Basic wards such as you describe, simply need the circle broken. In my experience, the problem is getting to the circle.

That aligned with what Megan had described. "OK. Sounds easy."

He stared at me. *Witches never make things easy. Don't forget that, pet.*

That I believed. Then something he said hit me. "You said, 'basic wards' what's not 'basic'?"

I got the impression of a mental shrug. *Witches can make their wards to do more than one thing, pet.*

That gave me a chill. What was I sending Megan into?

"What do witches usually make their circles out of?"

He blinked. *Usually smelly stuff. Things they use in their potions and such. I don't know specifics.*

Of course, a cat would notice smells. That made sense. "Any ever use paint in your experience?"

He licked a paw and chewed around the claw. Once he was satisfied he'd cleaned whatever was stuck on there—I shuddered at the thought—he answered, *Not in my experience, but this is a different age. They could have adapted to the times.*

Not what I wanted to hear. I looked at Megan. "Did you hear all that?"

"Yeah, but we won't know unless we try. We don't even know if I can cross the ward, so no sense worrying about what else it can do, or if I can destroy it until we try."

There was a certain logic to that. Even if it was the wrong kind.

Chapter Nineteen

I was ready to pounce on Luke when he pulled up to the house. How dare he put these ideas in Megan's head? She had nothing to protect herself with if she made it through the ward. However, I should have known that he wouldn't be that thrilled about the idea either. This was pure Megan. He was trying to dissuade her before I got up close enough to chew him out. So, I didn't light into him.

"I'm going to do it," Megan said, with finality, and put up a hand to stop any further argument.

Luke wilted. I recognized that look, he'd given in to her will. Since I'd already folded, I couldn't really get mad at him for doing so. Short of tying her up, we had no way to stop her, and if we did that, we weren't any better than Sofia.

It was supposed to be Megan, me, the Whelans, and a few other members of their pack. I didn't know their names. I'd feel safer with Mr. Mittens, but he had no real power off the land. So hopefully, things worked out in Megan's favor. Frankly, I hoped she couldn't get in.

Luke drove, and Megan and I crammed into the front of the work truck next to him.

"Are the others meeting us?" I asked after we pulled onto the highway.

"No," Luke answered. "They are out on a job, but they'll keep their phones close if we need backup."

We drove in silence, mainly because Luke and I had lost, and Megan wasn't listening to any more arguments. The warehouse was on the north end of town, I lived south of town, so it was about a fifteen-minute drive and some winding through town to get there. Kilchis wasn't very big, so our "industrial" area was also small—a few warehouses, a logging yard, a boatyard, and a combination boat repair and dealership were all that surrounded it. The road on one side and the sea on the other left little space for any greenery or trees, so the warehouse was fully visible if you wanted to look for it. I wondered why the witches met here.

Maybe it was cheap and large enough to host their coven meetings? Maybe they had a share in either a boating or logging business? I had no idea. I knew that Sofia had some kind of high-powered job, but that didn't mesh with the kind of businesses in this area, so maybe she did something outside of the coven. When we'd been friends, she'd been vague about her job and hadn't wanted to talk about it. She'd hinted that she was in charge of a lot of money and people, but no clue in what area of business. She could be a glorified fishmonger for all I knew.

We pulled up and parked at an adjoining business so we wouldn't be noticed. We probably should have brought Megan's car, because "Whelan Restoration" was splashed all over Luke's truck. Oh well, this is why we weren't professional investigators. We clambered out and walked over to the witches' warehouse. When we got within two feet, I could feel the ward humming. I reached out a hand and bumped into a solid, cold surface.

"I can feel it," I said. But it was obvious that I'd stopped. Luke walked until he ran into the ward, and then he growled deep in his throat. That's right, werewolf. I threw him a sidelong glance; it was hard to remember that not everyone I knew these days was human—including me.

Megan was three paces behind Luke. I looked at her, and although her face was set and her eyes hard, her hands were trembling. I knew she was terrified. Maybe our arguments had set in some.

She paused and straightened her clothes as though she were only going in for a job interview. Instead of trying the ward on the wall, we'd stopped at a spot which was devoid of windows, she walked around to the front entrance and marched up to the front door—a glass, two-door entrance that was a common sight around here. There was an open sign in the doorway, so at least she'd have an excuse once she went inside. This must be one of the witches' businesses after all. I wondered what they really did inside.

She handed me her alexandrite pendant, just in case—more shivers and bad vibes passed over me as her meager protection evaporated. She passed through the ward. I wondered for a moment if that meant the main door wasn't warded. It was a business after all, but when I approached wrapped in my shadow magic, I was still rebuffed. I slunk back to the truck which was positioned so we could see the door.

She went inside and disappeared. Now, we waited. She was going to text us if she got the ward down, and then we were going to sneak inside. If she couldn't get it down, she was going to do whatever spying she could without getting caught. I hated to wait. I wished Mr. Mittens were here, but he probably couldn't get through the ward either. Minutes ticked by.

After I checked my phone for approximately the three-hundredth time, she came strolling out. She looked normal, not frazzled or upset, and my heart leapt in joy. She was safe.

I wanted to leap out of the truck and grab her, but instead, I waited until she was in the truck to hear what had happened.

She shut the door and then sunk into the seat. "That was terrifying."

I gave her back the pendant with a sigh of relief. She fastened it back on. Luke reached out and grasped her hand over my lap in the close quarters of the bench seat of the work truck. He held onto her for a moment before letting go.

"So, what happened?" I asked a little impatiently.

She grabbed her water bottle from the drink holder and took a long drink. "The front is normal, like any business, complete with a receptionist up front filing her nails. It's like they don't know what a real business should look like, so they used a stereotypical one from the media." She dismissed their foolishness with a wave of her hand.

"I told her I had an appointment and just breezed past her. She barely looked up and didn't protest, which struck me as odd. Maybe she's an illusion or construct or something."

I didn't know if those were possible on that scale, but neither did Megan so I just grinned and waited.

"I went to the back, looking for the witches' circle so I could break the ward spell. I found the door into the warehouse proper; the front was just a few offices and a unisex bathroom. I looked back there, but it was full of witches. I mean *full*." She emphasized the lack of space by spreading her arms and crowding us more.

"I looked around, but couldn't see where the circle was, but there were so many people I could have easily missed it. I walked into the back room and slunk around the walls where it was darker. Everyone was so busy, I didn't think I'd be seen. There were stairs to a loft and more offices. I figured I could see better looking down, so once I located the stairs, I headed there. The stairs were your typical industrial metal steps, nothing aesthetically pleasing at all."

"And…" I tried to hurry her, but she was taking another drink.

"And I went up to them. Duh."

I rolled my eyes at her. "Come on, Megan, what did you see?"

"I could see the offices were dark, so I figured no one was up there, which was good since there was nowhere to hide, and if anyone looked up, they'd see me. And I stood out. They were all wearing dark blue coveralls, and hair nets, because they were processing fish. It stunk in there, I'll tell you."

That explained what business the coven worked in. Maybe Sofia *was* a glorified fishmonger, huh? Since Megan was wearing stylish jeans and a long-sleeved t-shirt, she would have stood out.

"So, I looked down. The circle wasn't literally a circle. It was just bits of stuff along the edges of the walls of the warehouse. Once I found it, I hurried back down where I wasn't so exposed, and snuck over to the edge of a wall to try and disrupt it. Unfortunately, even though the stuff looked like it was loose, it was stuck pretty tight in some kind of adhesive. It must have taken the witches a long time to make the thing. I did break it up, I think, but I won't know until you get close enough to try to get through it. I would have texted, but someone saw me, and I had to put on my act and be 'lost.' That's when I left."

"No one tried to attack you?" Luke asked.

"I'm here and fine, I think."

"Yeah, still that's scary. I should probably see if I can sense any witch magic on you before we do anything else," I said.

"You know how to do that?" Megan asked incredulously.

"No, but I think I can. I've sensed witch magic before." I was thinking of the gris gris bag and its foul contents, as well as Mr. Mittens hint that wards could do more than one thing.

"OK, sense away!" she said and closed her eyes.

I snorted. "Is there a reason you need to close your eyes?"

She opened one and peered at me. "Yes? I'm concentrating."

I laughed and reached out with my senses. It took a while to clear my mind, and I did end up closing my eyes, but I finally could feel a little something. I opened my eyes. "Turn around," I ordered her.

She frowned. "What's wrong?"

"There's something on your back, just turn around and I'll look."

She tried to twist around, but it was too tight in the truck. We climbed back out and once Megan's back was to me, I brushed away her hair. Holding my hand an inch away from her clothing, I felt all over until I sensed the sharp ping of witch magic. I plucked something from her shirt and held it out for her and Luke to see.

"What is it?" Megan asked.

I didn't know, so I shrugged. "A magical bug, I guess."

It did resemble a bug, but not anything I'd ever seen. It was dark green with an iridescent shimmer, and it had six legs like a real bug, but those appeared more for gripping than movement. It didn't have eyes, wings, or antennae, so I knew it wasn't a living thing. It gave off a slight magical pulse, and when I looked at it with my senses, it was a small thing, nothing too complex. It probably was just a homing beacon.

After we examined it, I tossed it in a bush and checked Megan over again. She was clean.

"Huh, I guess the ward did do more than one thing. Kept out the magical and marked any non-magic types with a bug," I said.

"Let's go see if that ward is still up," I announced, and we slunk over to the windowless wall to test it. Sure enough, I could touch the warehouse now without anything holding me back. The ward was broken.

"Good work!" I told her.

She beamed and buffed her nails on her shirt and then looked at them. "That's right, I'm your secret weapon."

I wanted to shake her because she could have died infiltrating the lair, but she had been successful and deserved to gloat a bit.

"Yeah, but it's still dangerous, and I don't want this to be a habit. What if instead of a tracker, they'd done something to you?" Luke asked.

I looked at him, he was falling for her, and he was truly concerned.

She recognized it too, because she threw her arms around his neck and gave him a firm kiss square on the mouth. "Thanks for caring about me."

Luke looked stunned. Like totally gobsmacked. I gathered they hadn't kissed before now, and I wanted to chuckle at the light pink blush that rose up his neck and over his cheeks.

He pulled her in close and returned the kiss with heat. I heard Megan gasp in surprise, and then groan deep in her throat as she returned the kiss with fervor.

I gave them a few seconds before I cleared my throat. "Ummm, I'm still here. And there are witches."

They broke apart.

"Yeah, witches," Luke repeated as though his mind wasn't quite back in his head.

"Let's go set up a listening device of our own," I said.

The plan was easy, if maybe stupid, but it's not like we had high tech listening devices to plant or magical bugs. We'd picked up some fancy game trail cameras with sound capability, and we were going to plant them in unnoticeable spots in and around the warehouse. The benefit of using them was they were easy to acquire, if pricey, they didn't require permits or anything fancy, and we'd get audio and visual information sent to our phone apps.

The problem was sneaking them inside and placing them somewhere no one would notice. At least we could all get inside now. Luke climbed a light pole and secured the first one, looking down on the warehouse parking lot and the front door. That one didn't have sound, mainly because all we'd hear would be road noise, and the beep-beep-beep of big trucks backing up. No one wanted that.

Once he was done, we were going to go back in to secure the others, which was the scary part. Sneaking past the receptionist wasn't going to work twice, I assumed, and the other entrances were for trucks at the back. Luke had suggested we wait for one, so Megan and I took our backpacks with the cameras and slunk around back to wait.

Luke went for fast food, mainly because he was hungry, and I could nervous eat anytime as could Megan. We found a place out of the way on some logs that were being used as a makeshift divider and sat. There were other people about since it was approaching the end of the workday. Some were going to their vehicles, and a few were also sitting on the logs, taking a break, so we fit in.

Luke came back a half hour later, and we sat and enjoyed our food, while waiting. Finally, a truck pulled around the back of the warehouse with a big reefer attached to keep the fish cool for wherever it was being transported. It started to back up. We had to time it right so we could enter before the driver came around back, or the crew inside lined up to transfer their fish boxes to the truck. It was going to be tricky.

Since I had my nifty new shadow magic, I volunteered to go up and give the all-clear for the others. I waited until no one was looking my way and wrapped myself in shadow. Megan gasped lightly when I disappeared from sight, so I knew I was invisible. I boldly walked up to the truck, hefted myself up to the unloading dock, and waited for the delivery door to open.

The big semi-truck backed up expertly, and once it was near, the rolling door opened, and I peered inside. A coven member was operating the door, but after it opened, he disappeared into the warehouse, probably to get his crew. I texted Luke and Megan, this was our chance.

They snuck around the building, hopefully out of the eyesight of the truck driver, but since he was busy backing up, that wouldn't be a problem until they were in view of his big mirrors. I hoped he wasn't nosy; there wasn't any way to avoid him seeing them if he cared.

I wished I knew how to include them in my invisibility

spell, but I was still a novice. Luke helped Megan up onto the loading dock, and then he easily jumped up. We slid inside the door just in time. A forklift was heading towards us, laden with fish boxes. We looked around for the best place to hide our cameras. There were some good areas, hard to see, but that would provide good coverage. But the best spot was a post near the main office where I was sure we'd get the best intel. The only problem was it could be clearly seen by everyone. This was going to be tricky enough with Luke and Megan fully visible. Placing it would be easy for me since I could keep myself unseen, but the camera would be highly visible. I waffled on whether or not to find another place for it.

Megan found the spot she wanted to place her camera and was slinking off behind some equipment. Luke looked after her, as though he wanted to follow, but then he went to his spot instead. I stood there, staring. It was the best place, and it would get the best information. I climbed the metal stairs so I could reach the pole.

Just as I got to the top, a door in one of the upper offices opened, and Sofia walked out. My breath caught, and unexpected fear froze me in my tracks. I knew she couldn't see me, but I was still terrified. She was standing three feet from me. I held my breath, irrationally.

A minion stepped out of the office after her and Sofia barked orders at the mousy coven member who was making notes on her electronic tablet. I looked for somewhere to hide before I remembered I was invisible.

"I need that information, now!" she barked at the poor minion.

"Yes, I'll be right back with it, sorry!" The poor mousy woman scurried away to get whatever information Sofia wanted.

Sofia was dressed impeccably as always in her power suit, makeup, and perfect hair. How could she work here and dress like that? It didn't seem practical. Probably why she never talked about it. Dress for the job you want, and all that. She sighed and looked over her kingdom from above, making sure everyone was busy. She frowned. Uh oh. I looked over the rail. Luke was clearly visible, and Sofia knew him. She knew all the Whelans. This wasn't good. Megan could hide in her anonymity, but Luke was too obvious.

She continued to scan, but her eyes didn't stop anywhere else but Luke.

I wanted to yell, "Run, Luke!" but that would give me away as well. The other cameras would be a bust, this one had to count. And now that I knew where her office was, I could simply place it there—where it would get the best info.

Since she was distracted by capturing Luke and because I couldn't do anything at the moment, I ducked into her office and looked for a good spot to hide the camera. It wasn't a huge thing, but a lot bigger than some fancy high-tech bug would be. I held it in my hand, weighing it, and wondering how I could place it. The corner of the office had some painted over pipes running through it, but it would stand out like a sore thumb. I dragged a chair over to the corner and tried to set it so you couldn't see it. That was a no go. It was just too obvious.

I sighed, and my heart beat faster. I had no idea how much time I had. It had to go here. I used the straps to belt it on and activated it. I stepped down and returned the chair. I looked up. I saw it plainly. Anyone who looked up would see it.

I was magical dammit. I should be able to conceal it. I

gathered my shadow magic into my hand, whispered at it to hide the camera and tossed it at the unsightly thing. It stuck, and the camera disappeared. Unfortunately, so did a section of the pipe. But it took a moment to notice, and that might work in our favor. I didn't have time to attempt to fix it or redo it, because the door opened, and I had to slip through before she closed it again. She was on her cell phone, so I slipped out before she slammed the door to her office. She was talking to security. I had to get to Luke before security did. I could probably hide him and Megan now.

I was so stupid, I should have tried this before we snuck in, but I'd been too hesitant and without confidence to do so. I spotted them from the railing and raced down the metal stairs. I couldn't hide the sound, and I accidentally bumped into the mousy woman on her way up, and she slammed into the railing and gave a loud, "Oomph." She looked around with wide eyes, but I was past her and gone before she could react.

I dodged through people and equipment before I made it to Luke.

"She knows we're here!" I said to him, and he started.

Invisible, I had to remember. "I'm going to try to hide you, so hold still for a moment, then we've gotta get out of here fast!"

"OK, do you see Megan?" Luke asked, but he held still.

I didn't answer, because I had to concentrate, but after I coated him in shadow, and he disappeared, I whispered, "Yes, she's over by the door, let's go."

We made our way back to the door where loading was still taking place. Megan was standing crouched behind the forklift, out of sight, but she wouldn't be that way for long. As soon as they finished, they'd want to go back for more.

I grasped her arm and whispered, "It's me," at the same

time so she wouldn't react. I assumed Luke was close by, but I couldn't see him. "If you hold still, I'll make you invisible, then we gotta go."

She nodded.

I concentrated and coated her in shadow. I started to see Luke faintly, so moving around was wearing the shadow magic away. Probably from me as well. We'd have to move fast. We headed back to the loading door. Just before we reached it, an alarm went off, and everyone froze.

"There is an intruder. Bring him to me," came over the loudspeaker.

Time was up.

Chapter Twenty

Luke jumped down first and helped both of us. We ran for the truck before all of our shadows disappeared. I hoped the shadow on the office camera kept it hidden. I assumed as long as no wind wore it away, it would stay invisible. But I had no idea, this was new to me.

We were panting when we piled into the truck. Sofia had seen Luke, so we knew the jig was up, but she hadn't caught us, and we hadn't been hit by any nasty spells. Luke started up the truck and pulled onto Hwy 101. While he drove, Megan looked up the app that connected with the cameras on her phone.

"Got it," she said once the real time feed connected.

"Well, what's happening?" I asked.

Luke grunted.

"Hold on, nothing yet."

She stuffed her earbuds in her ears since the truck and road noise were keeping her from overhearing anything important.

She held up a finger. "Sofia is *pissed.*" Megan laughed. She was quiet some more.

"Ooo, this is good." Another stretch of silence, and Megan's face turned glum. "Shit."

"What?" The suspense was getting to me.

"Hold on," she said impatiently.

We waited a while longer, town coming into view, then we were out and headed out to my house.

"Turn around," Megan yelled suddenly. Luke checked his mirrors and swerved to the right, hard, swinging wide so he could make a left-hand turn and not have to back up on the narrow highway.

After he'd completed the turn, our hearts racing, I yelled, "What's going on?"

"She's going after Gabe at the clinic. We gotta get there first. Call Gabe and warn him. I'll call Noah."

I pulled out my phone and dialed Gabe's cell. No answer. He was probably with a patient. I tried the office, but they sent me to his voicemail. I left a text and hoped he'd see it soon.

"I couldn't get him, what about Noah?" I asked her after I hung up.

"He's still out of town, but he's heading in. He'll be there, eventually."

We were silent the rest of the way, worried we wouldn't make it in time to beat Sofia and the coven. They already had people in position. People who worked there. Maybe it was too late already, Gabe wasn't answering. I took a panicked breath. No. That kind of thinking wouldn't help. He was just with a patient. He was a doctor.

I tried to calm my breathing and my heart, but it wasn't working. Megan reached out and grabbed my hand. I squeezed gently in gratitude.

"We've got this, it'll be OK, we'll arrive in time," she chanted softly to me. Probably to convince herself as well as me.

Luke pulled up to the clinic, and we jumped out. The clinic was a large, ugly tan and brown building in the shape of a U. It was two stories high and housed doctors' offices, instacare, the lab, and the imaging departments. We skirted around the instacare door and marched into the clinic. We were stopped by two receptionists at the front desk, demanding our appointment information.

I looked at Luke and Megan. "Umm, I'm here to see Dr. Ambrose?" I said uncertainly.

"What's your name and date of birth?"

"I don't have an appointment; this is a personal question. If you could just page him, I'd appreciate it."

The receptionist gave me a hard look, turned and whispered to the other lady, and smiled knowingly at me. "Is the doctor expecting you to call?"

This was a trap. If I said no, she'd dismiss me coldly. If I said yes, she'd make me wait until Gabe was free, and then go ask him. We didn't have time for either.

"Look, this is very important. Could you just ask him?" I begged.

"Dr. Ambrose is extremely busy with patients. If you want to leave a message, I'll be sure he gets it when he's free."

Yup, she was writing me off. I'm sure that Gabe had women throwing themselves at him. He was handsome, single, straight, and a doctor, but this was truly important—a matter of his life and freedom. I needed her to listen to me.

"Look." I glanced at her name tag. "Evelyn. If Dr. Ambrose does not get this information, soon, it will be upsetting for him. I only need a moment. Then I'll leave." I left out the part where I was going to take him with me. "If he doesn't get it, it could mean life and death."

She squinted at me. "Who are you? Are you here from the lab?"

I wondered why she'd jumped to that. I wasn't wearing scrubs, or a white coat, or any type of badge or identification. But, since she brought it up, why not? "Sure." I smiled sweetly.

"Is this about the patient I sent over this morning?"

I sure hoped I wasn't about to cause someone heartache or harm, but I said, "Yes."

"Hang on, and I'll see if he's available, Ms.....?

"Donovan."

She nodded and pressed buttons on her complicated office phone. I watched like a hawk. She waited. "Doctor, I have a Ms. Donovan here with some test results? She'd like to speak to you if you are free for a few moments? You are? OK, I'll send her back."

She waved me towards a closed door, and I opened it and walked through. Luke and Megan settled themselves in the waiting room chairs as I closed the door behind me and headed down the corridor. Before I had to choose a room or run out of the hallway, Gabe stepped out and gestured for me to join him in a room about halfway down.

"Gabe!" I said a little louder than I intended. My adrenaline was up after the ordeal with the receptionist.

"What's wrong?" Gabe asked, frowning. "What test results?" His brows were drawn together in confusion.

"I don't know about test results; your receptionist just started asking me questions, and I said, 'yes,' so she'd let me come back here." I took a deep breath. "We were spying on

Sofia, and she's sending witches here now to put you back under the spell. We gotta go!"

I reached for his hand. He looked at me for a moment. "I have a patient waiting in the next room. I can't leave yet."

"Can anyone fill in for you? I don't know what'll happen if she catches you."

He stiffened. "Yeah." He rubbed the back of his neck. A gesture I recognized from when we were kids, he'd do it any time he was uncertain.

He thought a moment more. "I'll inform the front that I'm leaving after this patient, and they can either reschedule, or I'll see if the PA can fill in for the last two of the day. I'll meet you in the parking lot in fifteen minutes."

I looked at him, "Are you sure?"

"Yeah, I can't walk out on the people in need, and I can't let the coven dictate my life," he said with a sigh.

I nodded. There wasn't anything else I could do. "OK, see you at the car."

I walked back to Megan and Luke. "He's going to meet us in the parking lot after this patient. Let's go wait by his car."

They stood and followed me out.

I leaned on Gabe's car; Luke and Megan were driving over from the other side of the parking lot to park nearby. I figured I'd have to wait fifteen minutes, since that's how long it seemed an average doctor's appointment went for something routine. After a minute or two, I saw the truck turning the corner to this part of the lot. And coming right at them was a streak of light. I opened my mouth to shout a warning, but they saw it. Both bailed out of the truck on opposite sides as whatever it was rammed directly into the front of the truck.

The truck exploded into a ball of light, and the blast pushed me back. I bounced off the hood of the car and rolled to the ground. My ears rang, and I felt as though someone had punched me in the chest. I groaned and rolled to my hands and knees to slowly stand up. My heart hammered, and terror blazed through me. Was Megan alive? Luke? Once on my feet, I swayed a moment before I could stumble forward to where the truck burned, a searing, white heat. This wasn't a natural fire.

Luke had shifted into his wolf. I gulped. We were blocked on one side by the fire, but anyone who looked from the other three sides would wonder what a huge wolf was doing in the parking lot of the local doctor's office, but he was standing over Megan protectively. I shuffled towards them until the disorientation from the blast passed, and then I ran towards my friend, lying motionless on the ground.

"Megan!" I yelled.

Luke growled and scanned the parking lot for whomever had attacked us. I got to her and bent over. She was breathing, but she had a smear of blood on her head. She must have hit it when she bailed out of the truck. Her eyes fluttered open.

"What happened?" she mumbled, and her hands moved to her head.

"We were attacked," I answered and helped her sit up.

Luke paced around.

I looked around briefly but didn't see anything. I could hear sirens in the distance, the fire must have been reported already. Megan stood slowly. I put my shoulder under her arm to support her, and she wobbled on her feet. Once I had her, Luke took off, his nose to the ground to find our attacker. I shuddered. It had to be a witch. That had been a ball of light, not a grenade, or a rocket. It'd been magic.

Plus, it was eating the metal of the truck. Soon nothing would be left of it but a scorch mark on the pavement.

If they hadn't bailed…I shivered again. I wouldn't think about it. We were vulnerable with only one side blocked from view. We needed to get out of here fast, before they aimed at us directly. I hurried, pushing Megan to limp along faster.

Luke's form meandered in and out of view as he wove through cars in the parking lot, silent and intent.

I pulled Megan next to Gabe's car, and we crouched down. We were in between two cars with a short space and the building behind us. Megan shook. I grasped her hand to give the little comfort I could. I pulled shadows around us to hide us further, but I'd just remembered to do it, so if anyone had seen us, they'd know we were still here.

I concentrated, for the first time using two of my magical abilities at once. Grabbing hold of my greatest offensive magic, lightning, I kept it in my mind, ready to strike. A slim, perfectly dressed figure stepped into view. Sofia. My teeth clacked together as I clenched them. The fury rising up and filling my body with rage.

I let go of Megan, tied off the shadow magic around her, and stepped into view. Sofia's eyes flicked to mine, and she grinned. Grinned. I let the lightning I held go and aimed it directly at her.

Chapter Twenty-One

The only sign she gave that she was surprised was a brief widening of her eyes, then she blocked my blast with an ice shield. I shook with rage. That was my ice. Mine. I sent a stream of fire at her, and the ice melted. She took a step back.

I smiled. This time, she couldn't out magic me. She was alone, and I was gaining better control daily. I sent another stream of fire at her. She paled. I called the lightning. I grasped it in my mind and focused. This time, I would hit her. I didn't care if it killed her at this point. I'd rather have my friends safe, than get back my piece of magic. But before I sent it after her, two more witches stepped into view.

Megan reached out and grasped my hand, trying to pull me back down between the cars. "Brigid, get down here!" she whispered urgently.

I sent the lightning at the three witches and ducked back down. I could fight one witch, but three? I wasn't crazy. They'd thoroughly kicked my ass the last time we met up.

Before my head sunk below the edge of the car, I saw Luke's grey fur shoot by behind the witches.

"Shit, Megan, Luke's behind them."

I couldn't see her behind the shadow shield, but her hand tightened on mine. "We can't let him stay out there alone."

I nodded. I wrapped the shadow around me as well, and we ran out, crossing the parking lot to the next row of cars —close to the witches. Sofia was barking out orders. They still hadn't seen Luke or us. Just then, Gabe strolled out of the back door and headed towards his car. He hesitated when he saw the burning truck in the parking lot, but before he could compute what was going on and react, Sofia spotted him.

Several things happened at once. The fire trucks turned off the main road and pulled into the parking lot, Gabe turned to look at them. Luke leapt up and hit one of the witches and rode him down to the ground. Sofia put up a hand and aimed a spell at Gabe, as I screamed a warning, followed by a blast of fire.

The fire truck took my blast, and my view was blocked as it passed by me. I sobbed out a cry of disbelief and anger. Once it passed me, I could see what had happened. Luke was lying on the pavement, unmoving, and Gabe and the witches were gone. I screamed in frustration. The shadows fell from us, and Megan ran to Luke. I followed, stunned. Sofia'd beaten me again.

Before we reached Luke, he'd shifted back. Megan ran over to the car and picked his clothes up off the ground. He was lying very still. I stared at his chest, willing him to breathe. I relaxed slightly when I realized he was. I reached out to touch his shoulder to make sure, and the moment I made contact, he leapt up and growled at me, his eyes aglow. I fell back on my ass with a yelp.

He apologized, and Megan handed him his clothes at the same time Luke and I realized he was naked, and my eyes were aimed directly at his junk. I looked away quickly. Megan took a little longer, I noticed, since my eyes went to her face. Once she looked away, she winked at me and grinned. I rolled my eyes at the total inappropriateness, but the humor eased the pain in my chest at losing Gabe again.

Luke hurriedly dressed between two cars, then helped me up off the ground. Since neither of them had a phone—as both phones were both currently cooking down to atoms with the rest of the truck—I handed mine to Luke, who dialed his brother to see how far away he was. Meanwhile, the firemen poured water ineffectually on the magically burning truck from a safe distance, while others kept the crowd away.

We wandered away from the action. Since there was nothing identifiable as belonging to the Whelans anymore, we acted like onlookers until Noah showed up with his company truck, and we piled in.

We filled him in again, and we all came to the consensus that the best thing to do would be to come at her when we knew when and where she would be. The full moon. The altar. My property.

The thought made my hands curl into tight fists, and the blood pound in my head. I wanted to punch her, pull her hair, make her pay. The thoughts disturbed me. I'd never been violent. I'd been the kind that took it and took it, mostly without complaint.

I was quiet the rest of the ride home. Megan kept throwing glances my way, knowing me all the way through, she knew I brooded when I was deep in it. I climbed out and let Megan say her goodbyes to Luke. I stomped into the house. Mr. Mittens was on the kitchen table, looking for all the world like he was expecting me to walk in the door at that moment. I stopped, startled.

"Hi," I said, glumly.

Something is wrong, he said.

I nodded and burst into tears. His eyes opened wider, briefly, then he ducked his head and gave me a firm head-butt. I scratched his ears, and he purred. The sound and vibration rumbled through me and after a few moments, I calmed down. A cat purr was magical in its own way. I leaned in and picked him up. He flopped over my shoulder, and I hugged him. Eventually, he gave a squiggle, so I put him down, and he rubbed against me.

Do you feel better? he asked.

"Yes, thanks."

What happened to make you so upset? He sat back on the table and curled his tail primly around his feet, his large eyes intent on my face.

I told him what had happened.

I will eat her, he said after I was done.

That made me smile finally. He meant it, too. There was no joking or doubt in his mental tone.

"I'll let you," I replied.

He huffed a little, not trusting my tone I supposed. *Tonight is the full moon, do you and the wolves have a plan?* He asked after a moment.

I shrugged; it was more of an outline than an actual plan. Sort of, get there first, take out witches, rescue Gabe, but I wanted my cat to think better of me, so I didn't say anything.

Hmpf.

I guess my shrug wasn't as reassuring as I thought.

This is what you will do.

Then my cat went on to present a devious plan. No wonder my property was clean of dangerous creatures.

I agreed, because what he presented was an actual plan, not just a vague outline full of hope. My job was to give everyone their assignments, so I contacted the wolves, Brightfeather, and Goch to do that. Then, I was to go conceal myself and Mr. Mittens ahead of time at the altar site. After I left a few magical traps behind as a diversion—nothing dangerous or difficult, just some light explosions to disorient the enemy—Mr. Mittens and I took up our hiding spots, and I concealed us with shadow.

This time, I didn't know what Sofia was up to other than putting the whammy back on Gabe. She didn't have me captured and couldn't steal my magic. I had it all except ice and air. Had she found my air magic? If not, she'd have to drag the rest out of my cold dead body.

She must have something up her sleeve, why else would she come back here? I shuddered. Something was going on, something we hadn't guessed at yet.

I stroked Mr. Mittens fur. I could feel the soft rumble that was his purr through my hand, but otherwise, he was nearly silent, waiting. Since the moon was reaching its zenith early in the evening, there was still some light when the witches started to gather. I hoped all was set up as we'd planned. As far as I knew, the others were readying themselves and waiting patiently for the signal.

The witches continued to show up. Even though we'd killed several, there must have been replacements, or more coven members were involved this time. It looked like the entire town was here to do whatever nasty thing Sofia had planned, however, it might just be that the clearing was now smaller since I'd regrown the surrounding forest. Finally, as more and more shuffled into the small clearing, Sofia arrived.

Like before, everyone was robed in a long black, hooded gown over their clothes. This time, Sofia's was decorated with silver thread along the edges. I couldn't see the design from my position, but I could see enough to differentiate her from the others. She directed the coven into their positions and had others lay out objects on the altar.

I realized my hands were clasped into fists. I forced them to relax, but it didn't prevent my heart from beating out of my chest, and the sweat from pouring off me. To make it worse, the finale of Sofia's conquest was being dragged into view. Gabe.

He was covered in a black robe. The only reason I knew it was him, was because I caught a flash of his face briefly, when his head flopped back, and his hood briefly fell from his face. Sofia barked something out, and two other coven members came forward, and together they lifted him onto the altar. He was much bigger than I, being over six feet and broad shouldered, so his legs dangled from the knees, and his arms hung over the sides. He must be out cold, because the position did not look remotely comfortable, and he wasn't moving.

It was growing darker. The sun had sunk below the trees, and I could feel the cool moon rising even through the clouds. I shivered. It wasn't at its zenith, so we still had time before whatever evil plan Sofia had formed would come to pass.

To make everything just that much more enjoyable, a cold rain started. I sighed. Although I couldn't see him, I imagined Mr. Mittens's face grew grumpier. Even non-earth cats hated water. I had on a rain jacket, and my boots, but still, the cold slithered down my neck and added to my discomfort.

"Bring the athame here," Sofia barked, and a hapless witch brought her a wooden box.

An athame was a knife. My eyes flew open. What was she going to do? Surely, she wouldn't kill Gabe? The coven needed him; *she* wanted him. If only to spite me.

She made the witch stand next to her and positioned others around. I realized they were all holding a wooden box. Were they all knives? I should have had her explain witch magic when we were friends, but I was too involved in my own magic and problems to ask.

Thirteen witches now surrounded the altar, Sofia, and Gabe. Thirteen witches holding thirteen wooden boxes of unknown contents. Sofia moved to the top of the altar. I'm sure directions were important, but I had no clue which way the altar faced, or if it was still the same as it was before I sunk it and reraised it. I hoped my changes screwed up her ritual. I grinned at that thought. Of course, the moon was rising in the east. Damn, why did I know that? That meant she was at the north end of the altar, and it was still true to the cardinal directions. What should I do? What were they up too?

The twilight was pouring purple shadows, and true dark was breathing down our necks. The coven members not in the inner circle were lighting honest to goodness fire burning torches to light the area, several more moved forward and lit a bonfire in the center of the clearing. I hadn't even noticed the brush pile there, hidden as it was behind black clad bodies. The flickering firelight added to the horrific ambience.

All the witches returned to their positions and turned toward Sofia, waiting. I realized I was holding my breath and let it out. Should I give the signal now? I wasn't sure. I asked Mr. Mittens and was rewarded with a gruff, *"Not yet."* The moon continued to rise in the sky, and I knew it wouldn't be long. Full dark had slammed down at some point that I hadn't noticed, since the firelight was keeping the clearing well lit. It looked to me like they were ready for whatever they were up to, so they weren't going to wait until the moon hit its zenith in a few hours.

Right as I was going to ask my cat for further advice, Sofia's voice rang out. "Brigid. I know you're here. Show yourself."

I shrank down, foolishly, I know, since I was invisible to her. I put my hand out to Mr. Mittens, and I could feel his muscles bunch up, ready to protect me.

She continued, "Brigid, I know you're listening." She paused for dramatic effect. "I knew I wouldn't have to do anything; you'd come to me."

What was she talking about? I wasn't going to hand over my magic. What did she think, I was stupid?

"You see, I don't need the doctor anymore. He's handy for the rest of the coven, but no longer necessary."

There was some confused muttering, but she silenced them, mumbling a few words I couldn't hear.

She gestured to one of the box bearing coven members, who came forward. She reached out, opened the box he was holding, and pulled out a long dagger.

I gulped. She held the knife high, so I'd be sure to see it. Its bright blade reflected the flickering light of the fire. She brought it back down and tried the edge with her thumb. "It's very sharp."

She stepped up to the altar and threw off Gabe's hood. She brushed the blade along his cheek like a straight razor, and I imagined the sound as it scraped along his whiskers.

"Sharp as a razor!"

Then she put the point at his throat. "This is what's going to happen." She kept the knife pointed at him and moved back to her place at the head. She had a better stabbing angle now, and my breath caught. "You have a few seconds to make a decision. Is your magic worth his life?"

I shook my head, although she couldn't see me, they'd never let Gabe go. I wasn't entirely sure she'd kill him, but I already knew I was going to walk right up to her and let her strip me of my heritage and birthright to save him from the slim chance she would.

I stood, and Mr. Mittens growled low in his throat. I let the shadow magic fade off of me, although I kept him covered. Gabe wasn't his responsibility.

"There you are." Sofia smiled her snake grin at me. She kept the athame at his throat. "Come on over, you know how this will go."

I did. She'd have us switch places, and she'd steal my magic. All of it this time. Why didn't I give the signal? I'd waited too long. I didn't see a way out of this, unless my allies were waiting and watching. We might have a shot while I switched spots with Gabe.

She showed more teeth. With her free hand, she gestured to the coven members, and they started to chant. My ears popped. I realized they'd raised a ward like they had the first time, and I cursed. My friends weren't able to get through it before, how were they going to now? Were they in position? I doubted it, I hadn't given them the signal. Shit.

I was close now, and two coven members grabbed me by the arms firmly so I couldn't escape. Mr. Mittens was still inside. I kept that thought as a beacon of hope. If he moved too suddenly though, the shadow around him would fade quickly. I had to trust he could take care of himself. Magic resistant, I reminded myself over and over so the fear for him didn't overwhelm me.

The witches dragged me towards the altar. Gabe was still lying there, Sofia's knife hovering over him. Were they going to move him and put me in his place? Could I use some of my magic to keep him from being stabbed? I searched through my arsenal of magic tricks. Water? Not much of a barrier. Fire? No, but I could throw it at the witches and hope they moved back. Earth? That was a possibility. Could I use my earth magic quickly enough so I could block Sofia before she stabbed Gabe? Maybe, but I'd have to time it right. I needed to wait for the switch.

They stopped me right in front of the altar, facing Sofia. The fire had made her hooded face look sinister, but now I was facing her, she was as perfect as ever. Her hood had fallen back, or she'd pushed it back in the time it had taken the witches to drag me forward, and her hair was twisted back in a perfect chignon, her makeup was flawless, and I'm sure that under the robe, she was dressed as immaculately as always. She liked to keep up the outward perfection. Probably to hide the hideous monster underneath.

Sofia used her non-knife hand to gesture that the coven members needed to remove Gabe.

He still wasn't moving except for the shallow rise and fall of his chest. What had they done to him? Was he drugged or under a spell? I stared at him, trying to read his face and search for magic, but I got nothing. So, not a spell.

I glared at Sofia. Four men came forward and grasped Gabe's limbs. Sofia stepped back momentarily and lowered the knife. Even if she never ate a carb and had a perfectly toned body, even her arm had to get tired. This was my chance. I reached out with my earth magic, and...nothing. I tried again, using my ring to focus, and only a tiny tendril responded. A slim stream of earth started to rise, and I dropped it. Whatever they were doing with the chanting had limited my magic. Damn, it had done that before. I'd have to break the active working to use my full power. I looked around, but I wasn't close enough to the outer ring of coven members.

Mr. Mittens! I yelled mentally. I hoped beyond hope that my weak magic would reach him. He'd have to stop them himself.

If you can hear me, take out the outer ring of witches! I can't use my magic! I kept yelling in my head over and over at him.

No reply.

I felt the helpless tears start to run down my cheeks, warm after the cold rain. This was it. No help was coming. Mr. Mittens either couldn't hear me, or he was also disabled by the magic dampening of the ward.

The four men dumped Gabe on the ground, out of the way. My breath caught, but he landed bonelessly, so I doubted he was hurt too badly. At least he was away from immediate danger, Sofia was now focused solely on me. I struggled and attempted to break free. The grip on my arms increased to painful levels, and I knew I'd be bruised. Once that didn't work, I used my lightning magic, and sent surges of shocks through my skin into their hands.

They dropped me, and I scurried back, but that didn't last. Sofia barked out a few words, and I was frozen in place. Not literally in ice, just unmoving. Try as I might, I couldn't move. I couldn't even blink.

"You didn't think we'd be prepared this time?" Sofia said, with triumph in her voice. "We are prepared for all of your tricks."

I threw all of my hatred into the stare I gave her.

"This time, there is no escape. Your friends are out there." She gestured with a sweeping movement of her hand. "You are in here, and entirely, at my mercy."

She said something, and I could move my head, blink, and take a breath.

I gasped for air for a moment.

"Any last words?" This was different. She'd also learned I didn't need my voice to activate my magic.

I looked around. "None of you think this is wrong? That killing an innocent person is evil? What is wrong with you?"

One person yelled out, "You aren't innocent, you're Fae. You don't deserve the power you've been given."

That was it in a nutshell. I wasn't going to reach them by appealing to their consciences, they didn't think of me as a person.

"Put her on the altar."

They lifted me like I weighed nothing and wasn't kicking and flailing and screaming with all my might. Probably because even though I sent the commands to my body, I was still held completely still by Sofia's spell.

Then, I felt the cold hard stone beneath me, and I was lying on the altar, staring up at the cloud covered moon, and Sofia's smarmy face. I spit up at her. It was the only defense I had left.

The spittle didn't even come near her but fell harmlessly back onto the altar beside me. Her smile increased.

The witches fell back into their positions. She nodded at them, and said, "Let's begin."

The witches of the inner circle began to chant. It was like I was being crushed in a vice. The chant was pressing in on me from every direction, and I panted with the pain of it all, unable to draw a full breath. Then when I thought I'd pass out from lack of air, I could feel the pull that was Sofia stealing the magic from me.

I screamed.

All hell broke loose.

There was a pop in my ears, like the change of altitude on a plane. The pressure ceased, and I drew a deep breath. I could move, so I sat up, and I saw what was happening. Mr. Mittens had transformed and was slaughtering witches. They ran around to escape him, but when they stopped chanting, the barrier came down, and my friends were free to come in.

Mr. Mittens was bad enough, but a fire-breathing dragon? The witches didn't stand a chance. They fled into the woods. Careful so he didn't set the place on fire, Goch kept to the clearing, but Brightfeather and the wolf pack had nothing to hinder them. I grinned and turned to see Sofia attempt to flee.

She wasn't getting away this time. I chased her. She had picked a random direction and was now running towards my house. Wrong choice. We slipped into the trees. Unfortunately, Sofia was a runner, and I was not, but I had the benefit of being on my own land. I connected with it flawlessly, using everything I had to cut her off.

Finally, I commanded the ground to block her, and she turned around to face me. Before I could say anything, she flung a barrage of ice darts at me, and I threw up a dirt shield to stop them. I hadn't thought fast enough to counter with fire, but at her second blast, I brought my fire up and blasted back.

She grinned, and I blanched. She muttered something, and I could feel her magic try to trap me again. This time she didn't have the coven's dampening field to help, so I shrugged that off and sent a lightning bolt at her. She blocked it with an ice shield.

We were evenly matched. I probably had more power at my call, but she knew how to use hers. I threw lightning, fire, water, and earth at her, and she blocked each spell. She tossed ice shards at me and spells that felt nasty, but I didn't recognize as I pushed them into the earth. The surrounding plants and trees blackened and rotted before our eyes. I was growing tired, and I figured Sofia had to be as well when Mr. Mittens stepped up next to me.

Sofia took a step back. She threw a hasty spell at him, and he walked through it. She blanched. His growl rumbled out from his massive chest, and she look frightened for the first time.

I'm going to eat you. He directed the thought at Sofia. I wasn't sure if she could hear him, but her eyes got a little wider. It could have just been his presence.

I put my hand up on his flank. To have him wait.

"What is your end game, Sofia? We were friends. Gabe would have filled your well if you'd just asked. Why do you have to hurt people?"

My questions came out soft and pleading. I flinched. I really did want to know. What was her motivation to do all of this at the cost of everyone that had been kind to her?

She stared at me like I had two heads. "Everything is easy for you, isn't it?" she sneered. "Born with life giving magic, a fearless protector, and wealth? I deserve some of that. Since fate won't give it to me, naturally, I've had to learn to do it myself."

She raised her hand and started flinging spells at me. I couldn't block them all. She fired them so quickly, I barely got up a barrier and couldn't think fast enough to throw back offensive magic at her. Spell after black spell struck the earthen wall, blasting it apart a little at a time. I was pouring my energy into keeping it erect. Eventually, her attack wore me down, and I sunk to my knees. The barrier crumbling. Mr. Mittens jumped in front of me to block the attack with his body, but even with natural spell resistance, he was getting hurt.

His help gave me some breathing space. I put a last burst of energy into the earthen wall to block her attack, and the second it went up, Megan ran to me from the side. She tried to pull me back into the shelter of the woods, but I couldn't leave Mr. Mittens, and I couldn't let Sofia get away. I gathered myself for one last desperate attempt. I launched myself at Sofia and landed on her. Both of our breath whooshed out, and she scrambled away from me. I hit the dirt, but before I did, I grabbed her by the hair. She fell off balance to her knees, and she lashed out with her fingernails, catching me across the face. I socked her in the jaw. Her head snapped back, and then forward. Her eyes flashed, and she snarled a spell at me. Megan reached out to put her hand over Sofia's mouth to stop whatever nasty thing she was flinging at me, I grabbed both of them. Mr. Mittens leapt at us, trying to get in between me and the spell. I grabbed at my magic. I didn't know what I wanted it to do, but it obeyed. There was a bright flash.

Chapter Twenty-Two

"Aargh." I groaned and sat up, clutching my head. It pounded with such force I swear it was going to blow apart. Plus, my face burned where Sofia's nails had raked it. My hands were on the soft grass or moss of the forest. I looked around. Megan and Mr. Mittens were sprawled with me. But something was off. I looked around for Sofia. She'd been right next to me.

She too was sprawled on the ground, but further away than I remembered. I blinked and tried to clear my head again. I checked that Megan and Mr. Mittens were breathing, then turned my attention to Sofia.

Her hair had half fallen out of its twist, and some was spread around her. I wondered why she never wore it down, it was long, shiny, and lush. Of course, it was currently a tangled mess, and her make-up was smeared. I smiled a brief grin at that. She'd hate being such a mess, I guessed she had to control every part of her existence. I shrugged. She was also breathing. I rolled over to my hands and knees and tried to stand. I staggered up, but my knees wouldn't hold me. I sagged and plopped back on my butt. Mr. Mittens stirred.

I reached out a hand to run down his spotted fur. He blinked his luminous eyes at me, then suddenly bolted up onto his feet.

How did we get here?

His mental question was loud and bounced around inside my head painfully.

"What are you talking about?" I groaned and clutched my head tighter.

Megan stirred and sat up slowly. "What happened?" she groaned. "My head hurts."

"Sofia was throwing a spell at me," I said, confused, and I…

The truth was I wasn't sure what I'd done. I'd gathered my magic up for a spell, and then released it. But I'd been wishing…

She's realm walked us to Faerie, Mr. Mittens finished.

"I what?" I asked stupidly.

He blinked his eyes at me. *You've taken us to Faerie.*

Sofia stirred. Then because she must have realized she was lying down, she sat up in a jolt and stared around at us. She brought her hands up in a defensive posture. I just stared at her.

I reached for my magic. Although I could feel it and the air seemed to tingle with the free magic of the realm, I couldn't touch it or bring it to bear. I tried again. Nothing. Sofia's face was confused as well.

"Mr. Mittens, why can't I use my magic?"

You realm walked without knowing that you have to guard yourself. Your magic was stripped away, and it will need time to recharge, he said simply.

"Grandfather and Dana never seem to have issues with their magic," I pointed out.

They know how to guard themselves. You have never been trained, he said with a mental shrug.

Story of my life. I sighed. Oh well, magic was new to me. I could live without it just fine. Sofia, however, continued to attempt spells, if her muttering was any indication, and was growing steadily angrier and more scared as she went.

"Are you OK?" I asked Mr. Mittens, sudden fear grasping me that I might have damaged him, my magical friend.

Yes, I've been realm walking for centuries, he replied, a little disgust at my question coming through his mental voice.

I breathed a sigh of relief. "Good, I was worried."

His gaze softened at that, then he turned to Sofia. He stalked towards her. She stood and ran into the woods. Mr. Mittens crouched as though he were going to chase after her, but then he turned his massive head at me. *Do you wish me to bring her back?* he asked.

I looked at him dumbly. "Uh, no."

He shrugged and gave me a wide cat grin. *She won't survive here long without magic.*

I'd worry about her after I took care of us.

I gulped. "How long before it…you know…comes back?" I asked nervously.

He gave me another kitty shrug, a sort of head bob. *It depends on the user. You, as a born Fae, probably a week or two, her? I don't know but could be a lot longer.*

"A week or two? Will we survive that long?" I shuddered.

He stared at me. Then in a blink, he morphed from his

true form to that of a tall man, with tawny golden hair and pointed ears.

I blinked at him. "Mr. Mittens?" I asked hesitantly.

"Yes," he answered with actual words. "This is my Fae form."

"I didn't know you could do other forms beside your Ragdoll and Splintercat forms."

"I'm a shapeshifter on all the realms that are infused with magic," he said. "I can only do the two forms on earth because the magic there is weak, outside of your land, that is."

"Oh." I didn't know what else to say.

"You've been here before. What should we do?"

Megan had been watching this all with wide eyes. She chose that moment to speak, as though everything had just registered through brain fog. "We're in Faerie? Faerie?" she repeated.

We nodded.

"This is so freaking cool!" she shouted and popped to her feet. "I'm standing on another world!" She danced a few steps and laughed. Then, she looked at Mr. Mittens.

"Why do I feel giddy, almost drunk?" she asked, puzzled.

I realized after she said it, that part of my disorientation was the same. A light tipsy feeling but with lots of energy behind it.

"This world is suffused with magic, and the air is purer, richer, than the air on earth," Mr. Mittens answered.

Megan sucked in a few deep breaths. "Sweet."

I heard something in the distance. "What's that?"

"Horses," Mr. Mittens said, alarm growing on his face.

"There are regular horses on this planet?" I asked, not registering his growing fear.

He nodded. "They come from here. Or the originals did, thousands of your years ago." He looked around, and sniffed, then as suddenly as he had before, he shifted into this Splintercat form. *We must run.*

"Run? Why?" I asked.

Because that group has felt our arrival, and they are coming for us.

I finally felt the fear that was emanating from him and spun to Megan in alarm. She grabbed my hand and dragged me after my cat. Afraid to speak out loud, I asked him questions as we pushed deeper into the strange wood. Now that I had really looked at it, the trees were slightly off from the trees of home. The color, deeper, the shape slightly different. Even the grass and sky were richer in color.

Who are they? I asked.

I don't know, but everyone here, everyone, has their own agenda, and you can trust no one.

What about my grandfather? I asked, alarmed.

We will try to make it to his lands.

Do you know the way? I huffed out, even the richer air wasn't making up for my lack of running ability.

Once I see a landmark, I'll know, he answered uncertainly.

Great.

The pounding of hooves was growing closer. Mr. Mittens was in front of me, and I ran into him when he stopped suddenly.

"What's wrong?" I moved around him, Megan behind me.

We've run out of woods, he said.

I could see that. In front of us was a lake and rolling green hills. On the other side of the lake rose a gleaming white castle.

"Whoa," Megan said.

"Is that a big enough landmark?" I added.

Yes, Mr. Mittens bit out.

He hesitated. The hoof beats were upon us, I turned, and I could see glimpses through the trees.

"Let's go down there, maybe they'll help!" I said, desperately.

Mr. Mittens sank onto his haunches, his head low. *In your colorful vernacular, we are thoroughly screwed.*

The horses burst from the trees and surrounded us. I looked up at them. They weren't horses, after a double take. They were centaurs, and they had us pinned down, their bows drawn and arrows pointed at us.

I nodded to Mr. Mittens. "Yes, we are."

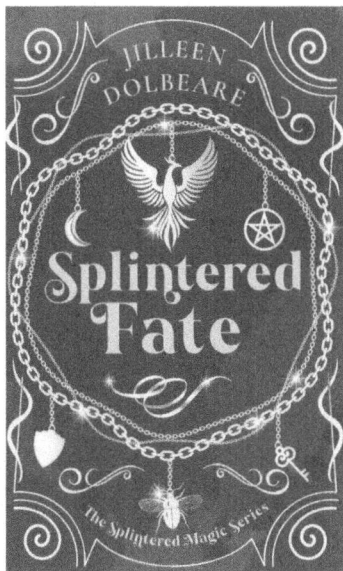

vinci-books.com/splinteredfate

Trapped in Faerie, hunted by witches—can Brigid reclaim her power and find her way home?

When Brigid's desperate gambit to defeat the witches backfires, she finds herself stranded in the treacherous realm of Faerie. With only her loyal cat and best friend by her side, she must navigate the labyrinthine politics of the Fae court, where one misstep could ignite a civil war. But they're not alone in this mystical exile— Sofia, the cunning head witch of the coven, has also been transported to this enchanted world.

Turn the page for a free preview…

Splintered Fate: Chapter One

The centaurs marched us by force down the hill towards a white castle gleaming in the sun. I dripped with sweat and shook with exhaustion and terror. Their weapons, mainly crossbows and spears, remained trained on the three of us. I'd always assumed centaurs would be mainly male, but these were all female. They were tall—their heads were probably two feet above mine—not that I was taller than average. I was surprised that their faces and what I could see of their torsos were remarkably human looking except for their ears, which were elongated and pointy—even sharper than the Lord of the Rings elves I kept waiting to see.

They wore intricately embossed, bright silver armor on their human torsos and their horse bodies as well. I wanted to take a closer look, but the fierce-looking leader kept us moving, and since I'd been poked once with a very sharp spear, I took it seriously—I wasn't sure if I should be regularly afraid or over the top terrified. I think I was a bit shocked that I'd accidentally realm walked us to Faerie. Who knew I had that kind of juice?

"What is that place?" I asked Mr. Mittens, who trotted along silently in front of me in his fearsome four-hundred-pound Splintercat form. The gleaming white castle looked gigantic in the light of the foreign sun.

It is the castle of the High King, he answered into my mind.

"The High King?" I trailed off when I stumbled and got poked again with the spear of the centaur apparently assigned to me. "Dammit." I yelled back at her, but she only poked me again.

"What do you think he'll do to us?" I whispered this time.

Mr. Mittens's mind voice was strained. *I do not know.*

"Do you think he knows my great-grandfather?" I continued to press.

Yes. He does.

That sent my mind on a tumble. I didn't know what to think about it. Did that mean they were friends? Enemies? Frenemies? I shivered. Megan bumped me from behind.

"Sorry," she mumbled.

I'd have reached back to comfort her, but I didn't dare. I already had three holes in me and didn't want a fourth. Who knew what kind of germs those wicked-looking spears had? At least they'd put away the crossbows. I could imagine the damage one of those would do if they went off accidentally—or on purpose. I shivered.

"What do they want with us?" Megan gasped behind me. We were marching along a well-used road and going a little faster than we were used to walking. It was hard on top of our general exhaustion.

"I don't know. Mr. Mittens said we are going to the castle of the High King."

Mr. Mittens didn't add anything.

Megan gave an exasperated sigh but didn't ask any more questions. She was probably also tired of getting poked and deep in her own set of worries. Mainly, what had she gotten into when she'd agreed to come to Oregon to help me?

I was worried for us, but part of my mind also worried about Sofia running loose in Faerie. What kind of mischief could she get up to, and what would it mean for us? I should have had Mr. Mittens eat her when we arrived, but I'd been too surprised, and a bit muddle headed from the air and the magic. Also, I wondered if Gabe was OK? I'd left him with the rest of the coven, unconscious and unable to take care of himself. Hopefully, Brightfeather, Goch, Noah, Luke, and the rest of the werewolves had helped him escape safely. I could only hope. Despair weighed me down, and my shoulders hunched.

With nothing much to do but wallow and walk, I studied the scenery and the back of the two centaurs in front of us. Faerie was lush and beautiful. The sun was warm, but not overpowering, and the green of the surrounding forests and grasses were intense. The breeze smelled of flowers and the sweetness of spring. In contrast, the centaur females were fierce and hard looking. They wore elaborate helmets that caught the light. The helmets looked more decorative than useful, since they left their ears free and didn't cover their cheeks or nose. The shine from the silver armor gleamed so much you could see them from space if Faerie had satellites. I had to blink and look away often to avoid blinding myself. The helmets and armor must be some kind of ceremonial wear I couldn't imagine sneaking up on an enemy in all that bling.

The centaurs in front of us also had long elaborate

braids under the helmets that swept down their backs like a horse's mane. Maybe that was the effect they were after, or maybe their hair actually did go down their backs like a horse's mane. The braids seemed secured to the armor, or their flesh, since the hair didn't sway back and forth as they walked. I wasn't close enough to see if the hair was attached to their backs or just secured to the armor.

Huh. If we weren't in terrible danger, I'd love to spend time studying these creatures. They were strange but majestic.

I stumbled again and got another poke for it. I took it back. They were not majestic, sadistic, maybe. I threw an angry glare at my poker but knew better than to swear at her again. She didn't even look at me. Hell, I didn't even know if we spoke the same language, or if they could even speak at all. We'd climbed a hill and were now looking down at the trail around the lake. It was lovely, well-maintained, and park-like. The trail seemed groomed, and the grass trimmed to an even length. The leader turned and headed down the hill.

They stopped us once and let us drink from the pristine waters of the lake. I tried not to worry about parasites or bacteria or anything else; I was too thirsty. Hopefully, being from a different world would protect us from the local infections. I looked through the crystal-clear water at the gem like rocks underneath the surface. A brightly colored fish sparkled in the depths. I might have smiled—I don't know for sure; I was too tired and scared—but the beauty around me kept surprising and delighting me regardless of the dangers. I scooped up water in my hands and drank what felt like a gallon. My thirst eased, I rinsed off the blood spots on my skin from getting poked, threw water in my face, and that was it. Time was up. The centaurs sped up and kept us marching until we reached the castle.

I took back my thought that this place *wasn't* like *The Lord of the Rings*. The architecture of the castle would fit right in. Lofty, sweeping, and ethereal, the intricate carving and design of the place was CGI worthy. It was so beautiful, and I yearned to be part of it. I couldn't even put into words the incredible spectacle it was. My mind wasn't clever enough to even create a place like this in a dream. It *was* Rivendell. Had Tolkien been here? Probably. Hope a centaur poked him. That's what he deserved for crushing my dreams about elves. I was still ticked that my grandfather hadn't looked like Legolas. Maybe I should be mad at Peter Jackson. *Hmmm.*

The walls were gleaming white like sun-bleached bone. I wanted to touch them, see what they were made of, but the centaurs kept us moving through the courtyard without pause. They finally stopped before a large, intricately carved door. It was covered with fantastical beasts and scenes that I didn't recognize—probably because I was on an unfamiliar world. Just as the doors began to open, I thought I caught a carving of some unicorns—the nasty bastards—but I wasn't allowed the time to study if that were true. On the other side of the door were more guards, two-footed this time, still in fancy shiny armor. They took over our care and marched us into the interior of the castle. At least we'd slowed down a little.

I looked at Megan. She looked at me. Fear reflected in her eyes, as I'm sure it did in mine. Mr. Mittens slowly shrank until he walked by us in his Ragdoll form, his glowing fur more noticeable on this magic rich planet. I wondered if that was emotion or design on his part. He'd been reserved since we'd been captured, and this made him seem scared. I'd *never* seen my cat afraid for himself before.

We were eventually ushered into a massive chamber. The ceilings were almost too high to be seen, and it was easily as spacious as an indoor professional sports arena. I looked around. People and unfamiliar creatures, wearing intricate robes in riotous colors and lush fabrics, milled around. The guards forced us forward. I stumbled and almost fell, but Megan grabbed my arm.

At the far end of the massive room, up on a dais, a robed and crowned figure sat. The High King, I assumed. I gulped. Megan slid her hand down my arm and grabbed my hand. Mr. Mittens's solid warmth pressed against my legs. He pressed on me so hard, I almost tripped again. We walked forward in our tight group, touching each other for comfort.

Finally, they stopped us and forced us to kneel before the dais. I trembled, as did Megan beside me. Mr. Mittens seemed smaller than his usual self, but when the king addressed him, he walked forward boldly, head and tail raised. I couldn't understand the king's words, and I felt a momentary panic, but then I realized his voice echoed in my mind and I could understand the meaning. I looked around. Did magic act like a universal translator here? I checked the ceiling. Was the room a universal translator? I didn't see anything that proved it *wasn't*.

"Xrsrphn, did we not banish you from this realm?" The King's voice was thunderous.

I thought I saw Mr. Mittens flinch. *Yes, sire.*

That was the reason he was so reluctant and afraid. Now that I knew he'd been banished, I was afraid for him. Would they take him away from me? Was this how they found us so quickly?

"Why are you here?" The king truly sounded as if he was curious. He didn't sound angry or accusatory. I felt a surge of relief.

I was brought here accidentally by my charge. His tail flicked at the tip, his anxiety palpable to me but probably not to others.

The King's gaze landed on us. He dismissed Megan, and the full weight of it landed on me.

"You are the progeny of my Pendragon?" he asked.

Was this a trick question? If he asked, he had to already know. He knew my cat and the terms of his banishment. Mr. Mittens had told me he was under a geas to protect my grandfather's progeny. So, that identified me immediately.

What was a Pendragon? I wasn't sure what that title meant here. I remembered that King Arthur's dad was Uther Pendragon. Did that make my grandfather a prince here? Wow, if that were true.

"Y-y-yes?" I stammered, uncertainly. I wondered if my single word was translated into the king's head as his were in mine.

He looked me up and down. Not the typical look you got from a man checking you out but an assessing look. And I didn't make the cut. I felt a teensy bit annoyed at that. Sure, I was a mess now, but I didn't think I was a total hag.

"Interesting."

I guess that answered my question about the universal translator.

His gaze flicked to a servant standing nearby. The servant hurried over. The king issued a command I couldn't hear, and the servant scurried off to fulfill it. I shifted my weight from foot to foot in nervous anticipation.

"What have you brought with you to my Kingdom?" he finally addressed me again.

I wasn't sure what he meant, and my face must have shown that because his gaze flicked to Megan and back.

"This is my friend, Megan," I said, not knowing what else he wanted.

"This is a *human*?" he asked, stumbling over the word "human" slightly.

"Yes, we both are," I added. Then I realized that might not be true. I wondered how much of me was actually human. By birth, I'd say I was an eighth Fae, seven-eighths human, but I had all of this power. I didn't really know what would show on a DNA test. Did Fae genes overwrite human ones? It was something I would only investigate in a private lab—if I owned one—once we were home.

He didn't answer for a moment, staring at us both. He looked remarkably similar to a human. Humanoid, for sure. Two arms, two legs, both races appeared similar in height. It was hard to tell since he was seated above us, but I'd put him at around six feet tall. He had long golden hair that was swept back. He did have slightly pointed ears, but I'd seen humans with equally pointed ears, so he could pass if he dressed like a modern human.

He was richly dressed in a long golden gown that was belted with a soft cord. Over that, he wore a large robe type garment that was made of some kind of fur. It was thick, white, and looked incredibly soft. He stood and walked down the three steps from his throne to us. Our guards straightened and became even more alert. They moved their weapons closer to us until the king waved them back. I breathed a sigh of relief. He came close enough to sniff us. Which he did. That startled me the most. I recoiled slightly, not enough to anger him, but enough he looked at me with surprise.

"You smell Fae," he said to me.

He sniffed Megan again, and his lip curled. He backed away. Just then, the servant that he'd sent came jogging back into the throne room. He cast about, looking for the king. When he spotted him, he hurried over.

"Sire, he is on his way." He then bowed and scraped his way back to where he'd stood originally.

The king glanced at us one more time and returned to his throne. He waved a dismissive hand, and we were guided back to a spot along the wall. Two guards remained, weapons trained on us, but we were forgotten for the moment.

People came and went, meeting with the king, but we were so absorbed watching and trying to figure out the local culture that we missed much of what the king was doing. I wondered what would happen to us, what the king would do to us when he remembered we were here.

It felt like hours that we stood there. If we slumped or looked like we would do more than shuffle our feet, the guards would force us back to attention. It was exhausting. I didn't even know I could get more tired, since I was exhausted *before* the centaurs had captured us. On top of it, my feet hurt and my back ached. I could tell that Megan was uncomfortable and tired as well. Even Mr. Mittens drooped a little. We'd been through a battle, a transport to another world, and a forced march over miles of varied terrain. We were too tired for this standing at attention crap.

Just before I burst into tears of exhaustion and frustration, the court stilled, and all the background noise stopped. I'd thought it was quiet considering all the people packed into this room before, but the deafening silence that followed proved me wrong. All eyes were drawn to the door we'd walked through initially. The door swung open, and a massive red-headed man walked in.

He was built like a brick—tall, solid, and menacing. His presence drew everyone's gaze like a moth to a flame. Even mine. He was in a shiny suit of linked mail, covered with hard leather armor. He had an ax strapped to his broad leather belt, along with a sword. It was a wonder he didn't clank when he walked or lose his drawers. I tittered. I'd had the same thought the first time I'd seen him. No way a *non*-magical belt was holding up all that metal. But since he wasn't walking bare-assed into the throne room, he must have a secret to keeping his pants up.

The crowd parted before him. My great-grandfather did not stop or slow until he stood before the throne.

He bowed his head respectfully but didn't kneel. I thought that was telling.

"Sire," he stated. "How may I serve you?" His voice boomed to every corner of the room. The crowd seemed to hold its breath and wait to see what would happen. Including me.

The king looked at my grandfather fondly. "I believe I have something of yours, my dear Pendragon," he stated and gestured to the guards. They grabbed Megan and me by our arms and roughly dragged us back to the throne. Mr. Mittens trailed in our wake. If they knew that Mr. Mittens was much scarier than us, they'd have rethought that move and grabbed him instead.

My grandfather frowned at me. Then looked away dismissively. My heart sank.

"Thank you, sire. I have no idea how this came to be. I'm very sorry to have troubled you," he said.

"No bother. My Scáthanna picked them up while training—once they felt the portal open and the presence of the cat. They needed the practice responding quickly to threats." Ah, that must be what the female centaurs were called. The king's tone was flippant, not bothered, and I sagged with relief on the inside. Maybe we weren't a big deal, and we'd be allowed to leave. I looked down at Mr. Mittens; he had sunk even closer to the ground and looked completely miserable.

This time, my grandfather gave a deep bow. "I am honored that you would watch over them, sire. I'll remove them from your gracious care."

"We will speak later." The king waved him and us away.

My grandfather froze briefly, then gestured at us. I grabbed Megan's hand and followed him closely—Mr. Mittens in tow. I could feel the concentrated worry and rage rolling off my grandfather's back as he walked stiffly in front of us and out the doors of the throne room. I'd really done it now. Feeling like a naughty child being picked up from school by an angry parent, I marched behind him. I was forty-two—way too old for this crap.

Splintered Fate: Chapter Two

We entered a room in the High King's castle. It was plain white like the rest of the building but contained nothing except an elaborate circle emblazoned on the floor and us. I reached a hand out to the wall; I still wanted to know what the material the palace was made of. The wall felt smooth and cool to the touch, like marble, but it wasn't marble. I frowned. I wasn't even sure if it was stone, bone, or a super hard wood. My grandfather waved for us to move inside the circle. We did. The circle was of a silvery metal with runes and hieroglyphs embedded in it. I wanted to lean down and touch it too, but I didn't have time. He closed his eyes briefly and mumbled something. A flash surrounded us. I blinked the light from my eyes and looked around. We were in a new but similar room, except the stone walls were now a silvery grey, rather than the white of the high king's palace. My grandfather strode forward, opened the door, and walked boldly down a corridor. We followed, not knowing what else to do.

He ushered us into a large room with a huge fireplace

and comfortable seating. One wall was floor to ceiling book-shelves complete with a rolling ladder, just like an old-fashioned library on Earth. There was also a heavy wooden table—carved and ornate. I'd call this a library or at least a private den or study if we were home. Megan was squeezing my hand painfully, probably as terrified as I was. At least we'd not been executed or accused of anything—yet. However, my grandfather was still holding back his anger, if his high color and flashing eyes were any indication.

"What are you doing here?" His voice was quiet, firm, and demanding all at once.

I looked at Megan; she looked at me. Mr. Mittens was standing extra quietly behind me, out of range, I assumed.

I cleared my throat. "Well, it wasn't intentional." I scuffed my feet, glancing up at him briefly before continuing. "Umm, we were fighting the witches. I think we were even coming out on top, but I panicked and accidentally brought us to Faerie. Now, I have no magic," I added as an afterthought. I threw up my hands.

"Hmpf," he said. That startled me. Did Mr. Mittens get that particular response from my great-grandfather or vice versa? Something to think about.

He was quiet, tension radiating from him. He turned his back to us and faced the fire. The fireplace was easily as tall as my grandfather and wider than my large sofa at home. You could roast a whole cow in it, if Faerie had cows—I didn't know. After a moment, he moved away, pulled out his ax and sword, and laid them on the heavy wooden table. He stretched his back. I was right, all that metal had to be uncomfortable. He loosened his wide, heavy sword belt and added it to the pile, along with the hard leather armor and shiny mail. Underneath, he wore a simple black high-necked tunic and pants.

Then he sat in a comfortable looking chair by the fire.

"Sit," he commanded.

We chose seats away from him on the opposite side of the fireplace and sat—none of us daring to disobey. He sighed loudly.

"You don't know what kind of position you have placed me in," he began, wearily.

I must have made a noise because he threw me a glance that would have shut up much scarier people than me. I shut up.

"The High King did me a favor. I will owe him."

I felt terrible. I had no idea what the favor would entail, but I hated anyone feeling like they had to do anything for me. I had some slight control issues.

"You do not understand our culture. I know that, and I didn't expect for you to come here until you were fully trained and cognizant of our ways."

That seemed more like he was talking to himself. But I hadn't *intended* for us to come here either.

"This is a dilemma. I'll have to present you formally at court. There will be other…repercussions. I might be able to delay until your magic regenerates. We'll see. I'm hoping the king forgets, but this was unusual enough, I'm afraid he will not."

I gulped. I had no idea what that meant or what it would mean for us, but my grandfather's worry terrified me.

His gaze swung to Mr. Mittens, who visibly flinched. "You have my permission to use your shifting magic in my presence during your time here."

Mr. Mittens looked relieved, like he was waiting for a blow, and it didn't come. He bowed his head and shifted back into the Fae form he'd shown us briefly when we landed in Faerie.

"Thank you, my lord," he said and gave a slight bow.

It was disconcerting to see my cat in this form. I knew he was a cat or cat adjacent, and seeing him with two arms and two legs threw me. His eyes stayed the same though; that was comforting. I noticed his feet were still bare and grinned to myself. He'd probably still sleep in the middle of the bed and jump in boxes. What had he done to anger the Fae?

"I must think on this," my grandfather said after a long pause. He pulled on a rope dangling near his chair, summoning a servant.

"Take them to the guest quarters, and send some food as well."

The servant bowed and gestured for us to follow.

Before I was sent to my bed, I turned and faced him. "What is a Pendragon?" I was curious, and I felt I must commit a small defiance.

He glanced at me, then away. "I'm the High King's Commander." Then he dismissed me with a wave of his hand.

Grab your copy...
vinci-books.com/splinteredfate

About the Author

Jilleen Dolbeare writes urban fantasy and paranormal women's fiction. She loves stories with strong women, adventure, and humor, with a side helping of myth and folklore.

While living in the Arctic, she learned to keep her stakes sharp for the 67 days of night. She talks to the ravens that follow her when she takes long walks with her cats in their stroller, and she's learned how to keep the wolves at bay.

Jilleen lives with her husband and two hungry cats in Alaska where she also discovered her love and admiration of the Alaska Native peoples and their folklore.